AF371655
THIS CALENDAR BELONGS TO:

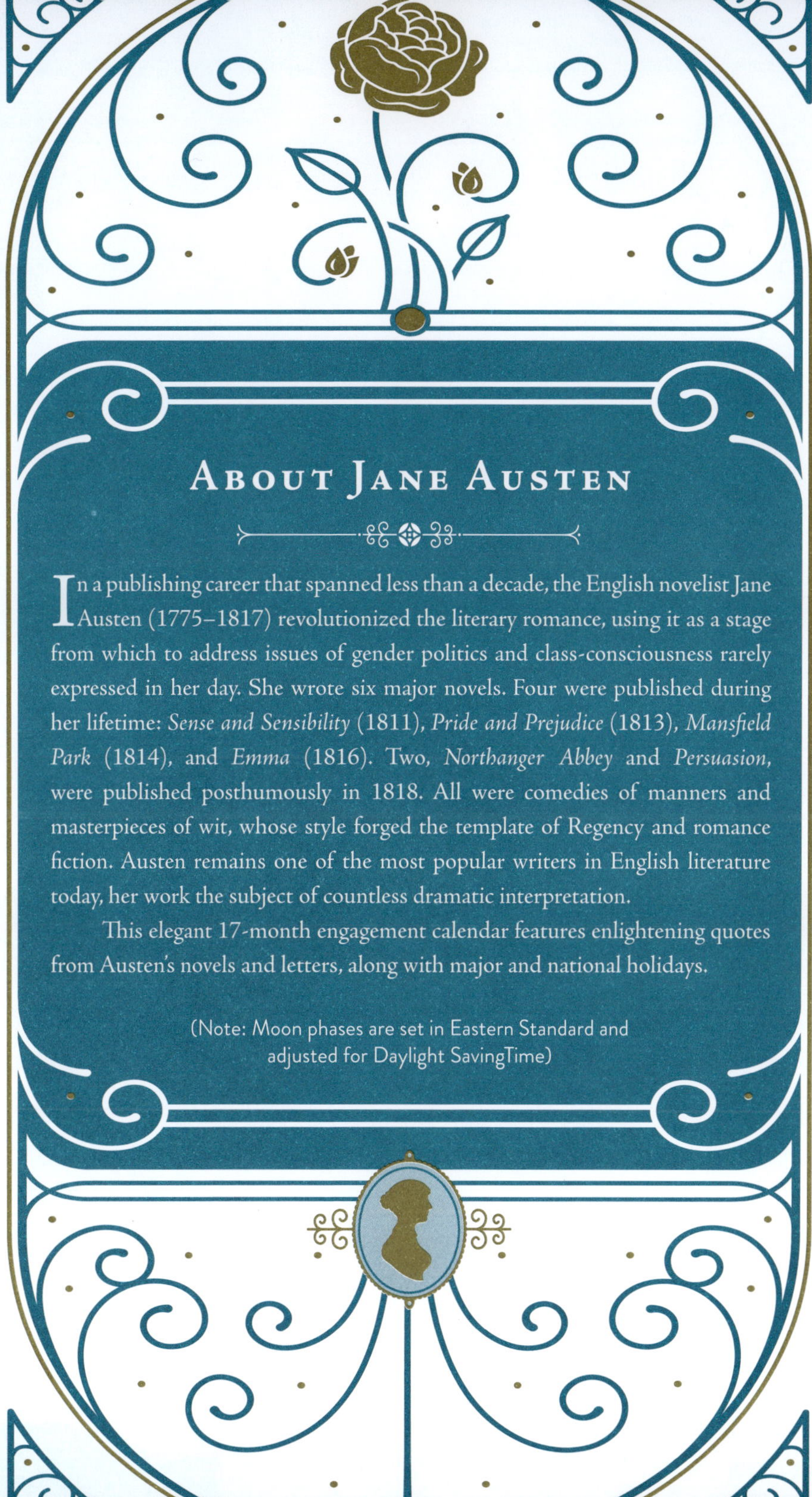

About Jane Austen

In a publishing career that spanned less than a decade, the English novelist Jane Austen (1775–1817) revolutionized the literary romance, using it as a stage from which to address issues of gender politics and class-consciousness rarely expressed in her day. She wrote six major novels. Four were published during her lifetime: *Sense and Sensibility* (1811), *Pride and Prejudice* (1813), *Mansfield Park* (1814), and *Emma* (1816). Two, *Northanger Abbey* and *Persuasion*, were published posthumously in 1818. All were comedies of manners and masterpieces of wit, whose style forged the template of Regency and romance fiction. Austen remains one of the most popular writers in English literature today, her work the subject of countless dramatic interpretation.

This elegant 17-month engagement calendar features enlightening quotes from Austen's novels and letters, along with major and national holidays.

(Note: Moon phases are set in Eastern Standard and adjusted for Daylight SavingTime)

AUGUST 2022

SUNDAY	MONDAY	TUESDAY	WEDNESDAY
31	1	2	3
7	8	9	10
14	15	16	17
21	22	23	24
28	29 *Summer bank holiday (UK)*	30	31

AUGUST 2022

THURSDAY	FRIDAY	SATURDAY
	5	6
	First Quarter Moon ◐	
11	12	13
Full Moon ○		
18	19	20
	Last Quarter Moon ◑	
25	26	27
		New Moon ●
	2	3

Monday 1

Tuesday 2

Wednesday 3

I wish, as well as everybody else, to be perfectly happy; but, like everybody else, it must be in my own way.

~ *Sense and Sensibility* (1811)

THURSDAY 4

FRIDAY 5

First Quarter Moon ◑

SATURDAY 6

SUNDAY 7

July 2022						
S	M	T	W	T	F	S
					1	2
3	4	5	6	7	8	9
10	11	12	13	14	15	16
17	18	19	20	21	22	23
24	25	26	27	28	29	30
31						

August 2022						
S	M	T	W	T	F	S
	1	2	3	4	5	6
7	8	9	10	11	12	13
14	15	16	17	18	19	20
21	22	23	24	25	26	27
28	29	30	31			

September 2022						
S	M	T	W	T	F	S
				1	2	3
4	5	6	7	8	9	10
11	12	13	14	15	16	17
18	19	20	21	22	23	24
25	26	27	28	29	30	

Monday 8

Tuesday 9

Wednesday 10

Here I am once more in this scene of dissipation and vice, and I begin already to find my morals corrupted.

~Letter to her sister Cassandra upon arriving in London in August 1796, from *Letters of Jane Austen* (1884)

THURSDAY 11

Full Moon ○

FRIDAY 12

SATURDAY 13

SUNDAY 14

July 2022

S	M	T	W	T	F	S
					1	2
3	4	5	6	7	8	9
10	11	12	13	14	15	16
17	18	19	20	21	22	23
24	25	26	27	28	29	30
31						

August 2022

S	M	T	W	T	F	S
	1	2	3	4	5	6
7	8	9	10	11	12	13
14	15	16	17	18	19	20
21	22	23	24	25	26	27
28	29	30	31			

September 2022

S	M	T	W	T	F	S
				1	2	3
4	5	6	7	8	9	10
11	12	13	14	15	16	17
18	19	20	21	22	23	24
25	26	27	28	29	30	

MONDAY 15

TUESDAY 16

WEDNESDAY 17

always deserve the best treatment because
I never put up with any other.

~Emma (1816)

Thursday 18

Friday 19

Last Quarter Moon ◑

Saturday 20

Sunday 21

July 2022						
S	M	T	W	T	F	S
					1	2
3	4	5	6	7	8	9
10	11	12	13	14	15	16
17	18	19	20	21	22	23
24	25	26	27	28	29	30
31						

August 2022						
S	M	T	W	T	F	S
	1	2	3	4	5	6
7	8	9	10	11	12	13
14	15	16	17	18	19	20
21	22	23	24	25	26	27
28	29	30	31			

September 2022						
S	M	T	W	T	F	S
				1	2	3
4	5	6	7	8	9	10
11	12	13	14	15	16	17
18	19	20	21	22	23	24
25	26	27	28	29	30	

MONDAY 22

TUESDAY 23

WEDNESDAY 24

We have all a better guide in ourselves, if we would attend
to it, than any other person can be.

~Mansfield Park (1814)

THURSDAY 25

FRIDAY 26

SATURDAY 27

New Moon ●

SUNDAY 28

July 2022						
S	M	T	W	T	F	S
					1	2
3	4	5	6	7	8	9
10	11	12	13	14	15	16
17	18	19	20	21	22	23
24	25	26	27	28	29	30
31						

August 2022						
S	M	T	W	T	F	S
	1	2	3	4	5	6
7	8	9	10	11	12	13
14	15	16	17	18	19	20
21	22	23	24	25	26	27
28	29	30	31			

September 2022						
S	M	T	W	T	F	S
				1	2	3
4	5	6	7	8	9	10
11	12	13	14	15	16	17
18	19	20	21	22	23	24
25	26	27	28	29	30	

MONDAY 29

Summer bank holiday (UK)

TUESDAY 30

WEDNESDAY 31

Full Moon ○

Laugh as much as you choose, but you will not laugh me out of my opinion.

~Pride and Prejudice (1813)

Thursday 1

Friday 2

Saturday 3

First Quarter Moon ◑

Sunday 4

July 2022						
S	M	T	W	T	F	S
					1	2
3	4	5	6	7	8	9
10	11	12	13	14	15	16
17	18	19	20	21	22	23
24	25	26	27	28	29	30
31						

August 2022						
S	M	T	W	T	F	S
	1	2	3	4	5	6
7	8	9	10	11	12	13
14	15	16	17	18	19	20
21	22	23	24	25	26	27
28	29	30	31			

September 2022						
S	M	T	W	T	F	S
				1	2	3
4	5	6	7	8	9	10
11	12	13	14	15	16	17
18	19	20	21	22	23	24
25	26	27	28	29	30	

SEPTEMBER 2022

SUNDAY	MONDAY	TUESDAY	WEDNESDAY
28	29	30	31
4	5 *Labor Day (US, CAN)*	6	7
11	12	13	14
18	19	20	21
25 *Rosh Hashanah* *(begins at sundown)* *New Moon* ●	26	27	28

SEPTEMBER 2022

THURSDAY	FRIDAY	SATURDAY
	2	3
		First Quarter Moon ◑
9	9	10
		Full Moon ○
5	16	17
		Last Quarter Moon ◐
2	23	24
9	30	1

MONDAY 5

Labor Day (US, CAN)

TUESDAY 6

WEDNESDAY 7

It was, perhaps, one of those cases in which advice is good or bad only as the event decides.

~Persuasion (1818)

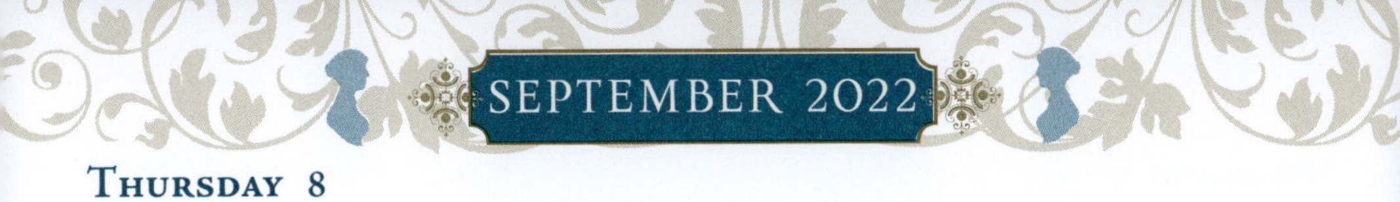

THURSDAY 8

FRIDAY 9

SATURDAY 10

Full Moon ○

SUNDAY 11

August 2022						
S	M	T	W	T	F	S
	1	2	3	4	5	6
7	8	9	10	11	12	13
14	15	16	17	18	19	20
21	22	23	24	25	26	27
28	29	30	31			

September 2022						
S	M	T	W	T	F	S
				1	2	3
4	5	6	7	8	9	10
11	12	13	14	15	16	17
18	19	20	21	22	23	24
25	26	27	28	29	30	

October 2022						
S	M	T	W	T	F	S
						1
2	3	4	5	6	7	8
9	10	11	12	13	14	15
16	17	18	19	20	21	22
23	24	25	26	27	28	29
30	31					

Monday 12

Tuesday 13

Wednesday 14

Full Moon ○

What dreadful hot weather we have! It keeps one in a
continual state of inelegance.

~Letter to Cassandra, September 18, 1796,
from *Letters of Jane Austen* (1884)

SEPTEMBER 2022

Thursday 15

Friday 16

Saturday 17

Last Quarter Moon ◑

Sunday 18

August 2022						
S	M	T	W	T	F	S
	1	2	3	4	5	6
7	8	9	10	11	12	13
14	15	16	17	18	19	20
21	22	23	24	25	26	27
28	29	30	31			

September 2022						
S	M	T	W	T	F	S
				1	2	3
4	5	6	7	8	9	10
11	12	13	14	15	16	17
18	19	20	21	22	23	24
25	26	27	28	29	30	

October 2022						
S	M	T	W	T	F	S
						1
2	3	4	5	6	7	8
9	10	11	12	13	14	15
16	17	18	19	20	21	22
23	24	25	26	27	28	29
30	31					

MONDAY 19

TUESDAY 20

WEDNESDAY 21

Full Moon ○

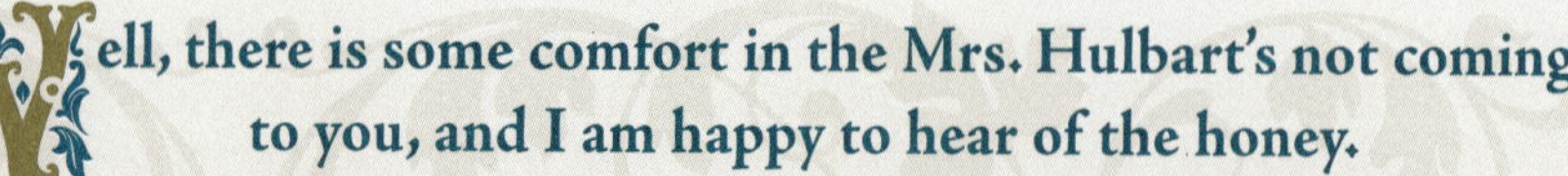

Well, there is some comfort in the Mrs. Hulbart's not coming to you, and I am happy to hear of the honey.

~Letter to Cassandra, September 23, 1813,
from Letters of Jane Austen (1884)

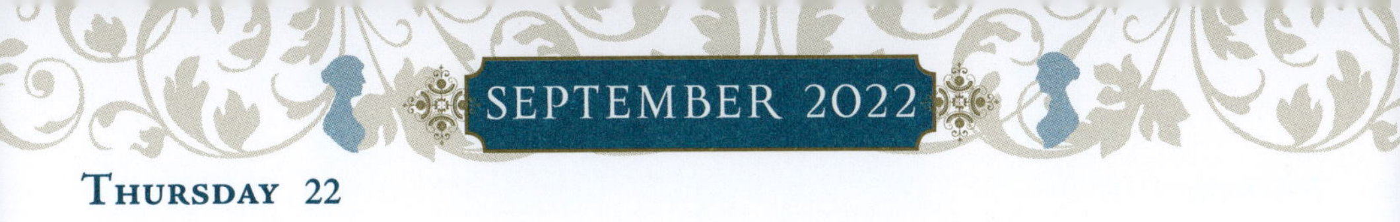

SEPTEMBER 2022

Thursday 22

Friday 23

Saturday 24

Sunday 25

Rosh Hashanah (begins at sundown)   New Moon ●

<table>
<tr><td colspan="7" align="center">August 2022</td></tr>
<tr><td>S</td><td>M</td><td>T</td><td>W</td><td>T</td><td>F</td><td>S</td></tr>
<tr><td></td><td>1</td><td>2</td><td>3</td><td>4</td><td>5</td><td>6</td></tr>
<tr><td>7</td><td>8</td><td>9</td><td>10</td><td>11</td><td>12</td><td>13</td></tr>
<tr><td>14</td><td>15</td><td>16</td><td>17</td><td>18</td><td>19</td><td>20</td></tr>
<tr><td>21</td><td>22</td><td>23</td><td>24</td><td>25</td><td>26</td><td>27</td></tr>
<tr><td>28</td><td>29</td><td>30</td><td>31</td><td></td><td></td><td></td></tr>
</table>

<table>
<tr><td colspan="7" align="center">September 2022</td></tr>
<tr><td>S</td><td>M</td><td>T</td><td>W</td><td>T</td><td>F</td><td>S</td></tr>
<tr><td></td><td></td><td></td><td></td><td>1</td><td>2</td><td>3</td></tr>
<tr><td>4</td><td>5</td><td>6</td><td>7</td><td>8</td><td>9</td><td>10</td></tr>
<tr><td>11</td><td>12</td><td>13</td><td>14</td><td>15</td><td>16</td><td>17</td></tr>
<tr><td>18</td><td>19</td><td>20</td><td>21</td><td>22</td><td>23</td><td>24</td></tr>
<tr><td>25</td><td>26</td><td>27</td><td>28</td><td>29</td><td>30</td><td></td></tr>
</table>

<table>
<tr><td colspan="7" align="center">October 2022</td></tr>
<tr><td>S</td><td>M</td><td>T</td><td>W</td><td>T</td><td>F</td><td>S</td></tr>
<tr><td></td><td></td><td></td><td></td><td></td><td></td><td>1</td></tr>
<tr><td>2</td><td>3</td><td>4</td><td>5</td><td>6</td><td>7</td><td>8</td></tr>
<tr><td>9</td><td>10</td><td>11</td><td>12</td><td>13</td><td>14</td><td>15</td></tr>
<tr><td>16</td><td>17</td><td>18</td><td>19</td><td>20</td><td>21</td><td>22</td></tr>
<tr><td>23</td><td>24</td><td>25</td><td>26</td><td>27</td><td>28</td><td>29</td></tr>
<tr><td>30</td><td>31</td><td></td><td></td><td></td><td></td><td></td></tr>
</table>

Monday 26

Tuesday 27

Wednesday 28

Full Moon ○

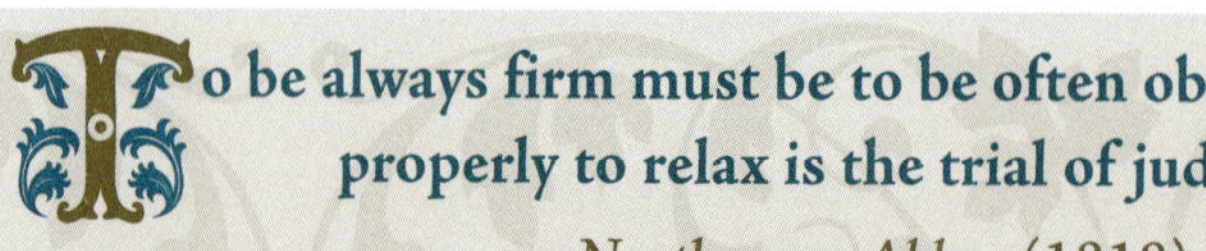

To be always firm must be to be often obstinate. When properly to relax is the trial of judgment.

~Northanger Abbey (1818)

Thursday 29

Friday 30

Saturday 1

Sunday 2

First Quarter Moon ◐

August 2022						
S	M	T	W	T	F	S
	1	2	3	4	5	6
7	8	9	10	11	12	13
14	15	16	17	18	19	20
21	22	23	24	25	26	27
28	29	30	31			

September 2022						
S	M	T	W	T	F	S
				1	2	3
4	5	6	7	8	9	10
11	12	13	14	15	16	17
18	19	20	21	22	23	24
25	26	27	28	29	30	

October 2022						
S	M	T	W	T	F	S
						1
2	3	4	5	6	7	8
9	10	11	12	13	14	15
16	17	18	19	20	21	22
23	24	25	26	27	28	29
30	31					

OCTOBER 2022

SUNDAY	MONDAY	TUESDAY	WEDNESDAY
25	26	27	28
2 *First Quarter Moon* ◑	3	4 *Yom Kippur* *(begins at sundown)*	5
9 *Full Moon* ○	10 *Indigenous Peoples' Day,* *Columbus Day (US),* *Thanksgiving (CAN)*	11	12
16	17 *Last Quarter Moon* ◐	18	19
23 / 30	24 / 31 *Halloween*	25 *New Moon* ●	26

OCTOBER 2022

THURSDAY	FRIDAY	SATURDAY
29	30	1
6	7	8
13	14	15
20	21	22
27	28	29

NOTES

Monday 3

Tuesday 4

Yom Kippur (begins at sundown)

Wednesday 5

Pray remember me to everybody who does not inquire after me; those who do, remember me without bidding.

~Letter to Cassandra, September 5, 1796,
from *Letters of Jane Austen* (1884)

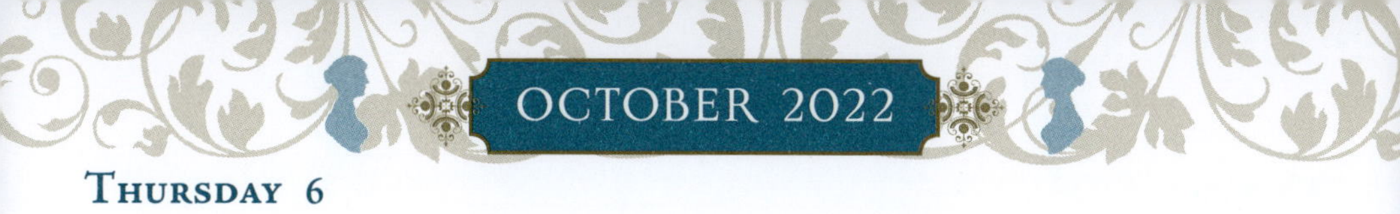

OCTOBER 2022

THURSDAY 6

FRIDAY 7

SATURDAY 8

SUNDAY 9

Full Moon ○

<table>
<tr><td colspan="7" align="center">September 2022</td></tr>
<tr><td>S</td><td>M</td><td>T</td><td>W</td><td>T</td><td>F</td><td>S</td></tr>
<tr><td></td><td></td><td></td><td></td><td>1</td><td>2</td><td>3</td></tr>
<tr><td>4</td><td>5</td><td>6</td><td>7</td><td>8</td><td>9</td><td>10</td></tr>
<tr><td>11</td><td>12</td><td>13</td><td>14</td><td>15</td><td>16</td><td>17</td></tr>
<tr><td>18</td><td>19</td><td>20</td><td>21</td><td>22</td><td>23</td><td>24</td></tr>
<tr><td>25</td><td>26</td><td>27</td><td>28</td><td>29</td><td>30</td><td></td></tr>
</table>

<table>
<tr><td colspan="7" align="center">October 2022</td></tr>
<tr><td>S</td><td>M</td><td>T</td><td>W</td><td>T</td><td>F</td><td>S</td></tr>
<tr><td></td><td></td><td></td><td></td><td></td><td></td><td>1</td></tr>
<tr><td>2</td><td>3</td><td>4</td><td>5</td><td>6</td><td>7</td><td>8</td></tr>
<tr><td>9</td><td>10</td><td>11</td><td>12</td><td>13</td><td>14</td><td>15</td></tr>
<tr><td>16</td><td>17</td><td>18</td><td>19</td><td>20</td><td>21</td><td>22</td></tr>
<tr><td>23</td><td>24</td><td>25</td><td>26</td><td>27</td><td>28</td><td>29</td></tr>
<tr><td>30</td><td>31</td><td></td><td></td><td></td><td></td><td></td></tr>
</table>

<table>
<tr><td colspan="7" align="center">November 2022</td></tr>
<tr><td>S</td><td>M</td><td>T</td><td>W</td><td>T</td><td>F</td><td>S</td></tr>
<tr><td></td><td></td><td>1</td><td>2</td><td>3</td><td>4</td><td>5</td></tr>
<tr><td>6</td><td>7</td><td>8</td><td>9</td><td>10</td><td>11</td><td>12</td></tr>
<tr><td>13</td><td>14</td><td>15</td><td>16</td><td>17</td><td>18</td><td>19</td></tr>
<tr><td>20</td><td>21</td><td>22</td><td>23</td><td>24</td><td>25</td><td>26</td></tr>
<tr><td>27</td><td>28</td><td>29</td><td>30</td><td></td><td></td><td></td></tr>
</table>

MONDAY 10

Indigenous Peoples' Day, Columbus Day (US), Thanksgiving (CAN)

TUESDAY 11

WEDNESDAY 12

I will be calm. I will be mistress of myself.
~Sense and Sensibility (1811)

Thursday 13

Friday 14

Saturday 15

Sunday 16

<table>
<tr><td colspan="7">September 2022</td></tr>
<tr><td>S</td><td>M</td><td>T</td><td>W</td><td>T</td><td>F</td><td>S</td></tr>
<tr><td></td><td></td><td></td><td></td><td>1</td><td>2</td><td>3</td></tr>
<tr><td>4</td><td>5</td><td>6</td><td>7</td><td>8</td><td>9</td><td>10</td></tr>
<tr><td>11</td><td>12</td><td>13</td><td>14</td><td>15</td><td>16</td><td>17</td></tr>
<tr><td>18</td><td>19</td><td>20</td><td>21</td><td>22</td><td>23</td><td>24</td></tr>
<tr><td>25</td><td>26</td><td>27</td><td>28</td><td>29</td><td>30</td><td></td></tr>
</table>

<table>
<tr><td colspan="7">October 2022</td></tr>
<tr><td>S</td><td>M</td><td>T</td><td>W</td><td>T</td><td>F</td><td>S</td></tr>
<tr><td></td><td></td><td></td><td></td><td></td><td></td><td>1</td></tr>
<tr><td>2</td><td>3</td><td>4</td><td>5</td><td>6</td><td>7</td><td>8</td></tr>
<tr><td>9</td><td>10</td><td>11</td><td>12</td><td>13</td><td>14</td><td>15</td></tr>
<tr><td>16</td><td>17</td><td>18</td><td>19</td><td>20</td><td>21</td><td>22</td></tr>
<tr><td>23</td><td>24</td><td>25</td><td>26</td><td>27</td><td>28</td><td>29</td></tr>
<tr><td>30</td><td>31</td><td></td><td></td><td></td><td></td><td></td></tr>
</table>

<table>
<tr><td colspan="7">November 2022</td></tr>
<tr><td>S</td><td>M</td><td>T</td><td>W</td><td>T</td><td>F</td><td>S</td></tr>
<tr><td></td><td></td><td>1</td><td>2</td><td>3</td><td>4</td><td>5</td></tr>
<tr><td>6</td><td>7</td><td>8</td><td>9</td><td>10</td><td>11</td><td>12</td></tr>
<tr><td>13</td><td>14</td><td>15</td><td>16</td><td>17</td><td>18</td><td>19</td></tr>
<tr><td>20</td><td>21</td><td>22</td><td>23</td><td>24</td><td>25</td><td>26</td></tr>
<tr><td>27</td><td>28</td><td>29</td><td>30</td><td></td><td></td><td></td></tr>
</table>

Monday 17

Last Quarter Moon ◗

Tuesday 18

Wednesday 19

Full Moon ○

There is a stubbornness about me that never can bear to be frightened at the will of others. My courage always rises at every attempt to intimidate me.

~*Pride and Prejudice* (1813)

Thursday 20

Friday 21

Saturday 22

Sunday 23

September 2022

S	M	T	W	T	F	S
				1	2	3
4	5	6	7	8	9	10
11	12	13	14	15	16	17
18	19	20	21	22	23	24
25	26	27	28	29	30	

October 2022

S	M	T	W	T	F	S
						1
2	3	4	5	6	7	8
9	10	11	12	13	14	15
16	17	18	19	20	21	22
23	24	25	26	27	28	29
30	31					

November 2022

S	M	T	W	T	F	S
		1	2	3	4	5
6	7	8	9	10	11	12
13	14	15	16	17	18	19
20	21	22	23	24	25	26
27	28	29	30			

MONDAY 24

TUESDAY 25

New Moon ●

WEDNESDAY 26

Next week I shall begin my operations on my hat, on which you know my principal hopes of happiness depend.

~Letter to Cassandra, October 27, 1798,
from *Letters of Jane Austen* (1884)

OCTOBER 2022

Thursday 27

Friday 28

Saturday 29

Sunday 30

September 2022						
S	M	T	W	T	F	S
				1	2	3
4	5	6	7	8	9	10
11	12	13	14	15	16	17
18	19	20	21	22	23	24
25	26	27	28	29	30	

October 2022						
S	M	T	W	T	F	S
						1
2	3	4	5	6	7	8
9	10	11	12	13	14	15
16	17	18	19	20	21	22
23	24	25	26	27	28	29
30	31					

November 2022						
S	M	T	W	T	F	S
		1	2	3	4	5
6	7	8	9	10	11	12
13	14	15	16	17	18	19
20	21	22	23	24	25	26
27	28	29	30			

NOVEMBER 2022

SUNDAY	MONDAY	TUESDAY	WEDNESDAY
30	31	1 *First Quarter Moon* ◑	2
6 *Daylight Saving Time Ends (US, CAN)*	7	8 *Election Day (US)* *Full Moon* ○	9
13	14	15	16 *Last Quarter Moon* ◖
20	21	22	23 *New Moon* ●
27	28	29	30 *First Quarter Moon* ◑

THURSDAY	FRIDAY	SATURDAY
	4	5
0	11	12
	Veterans Day (US)	
7	18	19
4	25	26
...hanksgiving (US)	2	3

NOTES

MONDAY 31

Halloween

TUESDAY 1

First Quarter Moon ◐

WEDNESDAY 2

A sound like receding footsteps and the closing of a distant door struck on her affrighted ear. Human nature could support no more.

~Northanger Abbey (1817)

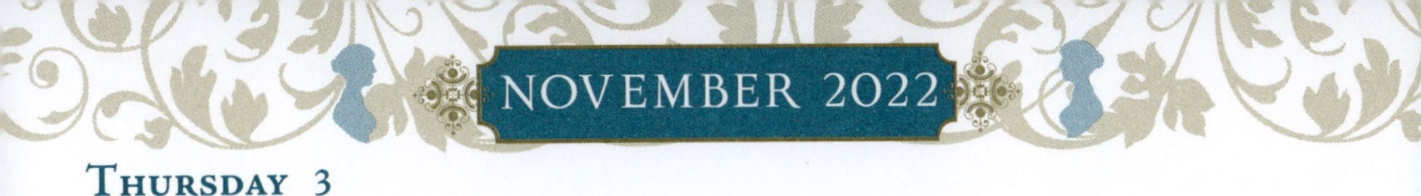

NOVEMBER 2022

THURSDAY 3

FRIDAY 4

SATURDAY 5

SUNDAY 6

Daylight Saving Time Ends (US, CAN)

October 2022						
S	M	T	W	T	F	S
						1
2	3	4	5	6	7	8
9	10	11	12	13	14	15
16	17	18	19	20	21	22
23	24	25	26	27	28	29
30	31					

November 2022						
S	M	T	W	T	F	S
		1	2	3	4	5
6	7	8	9	10	11	12
13	14	15	16	17	18	19
20	21	22	23	24	25	26
27	28	29	30			

December 2023						
S	M	T	W	T	F	S
					1	2
3	4	5	6	7	8	9
10	11	12	13	14	15	16
17	18	19	20	21	22	23
24	25	26	27	28	29	30
31						

MONDAY 7

TUESDAY 8

Election Day (US)   *Full Moon* ○

WEDNESDAY 9

speak what appears to me the general opinion; and where an opinion is general, it is usually correct.

~Mansfield Park (1814)

THURSDAY 10

FRIDAY 11

Veterans Day (US)

SATURDAY 12

October 2022						
S	M	T	W	T	F	S
						1
2	3	4	5	6	7	8
9	10	11	12	13	14	15
16	17	18	19	20	21	22
23	24	25	26	27	28	29
30	31					

November 2022						
S	M	T	W	T	F	S
		1	2	3	4	5
6	7	8	9	10	11	12
13	14	15	16	17	18	19
20	21	22	23	24	25	26
27	28	29	30			

SUNDAY 13

December 2023						
S	M	T	W	T	F	S
					1	2	3
4	5	6	7	8	9	10
11	12	13	14	15	16	17
18	19	20	21	22	23	24
25	26	27	28	29	30	31

Monday 14

Tuesday 15

Wednesday 16

Last Quarter Moon ◑

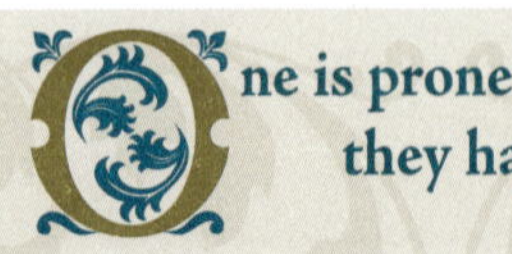

One is prone to think much more of such things the morning after they happen, than when time has entirely driven them out of one's recollection.

~Letter to Cassandra, November 20, 1800, from *Letters of Jane Austen* (1884)

NOVEMBER 2022

THURSDAY 17

FRIDAY 18

SATURDAY 19

SUNDAY 20

October 2022

S	M	T	W	T	F	S
						1
2	3	4	5	6	7	8
9	10	11	12	13	14	15
16	17	18	19	20	21	22
23	24	25	26	27	28	29
30	31					

November 2022

S	M	T	W	T	F	S
		1	2	3	4	5
6	7	8	9	10	11	12
13	14	15	16	17	18	19
20	21	22	23	24	25	26
27	28	29	30			

December 2023

S	M	T	W	T	F	S
					1	2	3
4	5	6	7	8	9	10
11	12	13	14	15	16	17
18	19	20	21	22	23	24
25	26	27	28	29	30	31

Monday 21

Tuesday 22

Wednesday 23

New Moon ●

How could you have a wet day on Thursday? With us it was a prince of days.... Everybody was out and talking of spring.

~Letter to Cassandra, November 21, 1808, from *Letters of Jane Austen* (1884)

Thursday 24

Thanksgiving (US)

Friday 25

Saturday 26

Sunday 27

October 2022						
S	M	T	W	T	F	S
						1
2	3	4	5	6	7	8
9	10	11	12	13	14	15
16	17	18	19	20	21	22
23	24	25	26	27	28	29
30	31					

November 2022						
S	M	T	W	T	F	S
		1	2	3	4	5
6	7	8	9	10	11	12
13	14	15	16	17	18	19
20	21	22	23	24	25	26
27	28	29	30			

December 2023						
S	M	T	W	T	F	S
					1	2
4	5	6	7	8	9	10
11	12	13	14	15	16	17
18	19	20	21	22	23	24
25	26	27	28	29	30	31

MONDAY 28

TUESDAY 29

WEDNESDAY 30

First Quarter Moon ◐

Ah! there is nothing like staying
at home for real comfort.
~*Emma* (1815)

DECEMBER 2022

Thursday 1

Friday 2

Saturday 3

Sunday 4

October 2022

S	M	T	W	T	F	S
						1
2	3	4	5	6	7	8
9	10	11	12	13	14	15
16	17	18	19	20	21	22
23	24	25	26	27	28	29
30	31					

November 2022

S	M	T	W	T	F	S
		1	2	3	4	5
6	7	8	9	10	11	12
13	14	15	16	17	18	19
20	21	22	23	24	25	26
27	28	29	30			

December 2023

S	M	T	W	T	F	S
					1	2	3
4	5	6	7	8	9	10
11	12	13	14	15	16	17
18	19	20	21	22	23	24
25	26	27	28	29	30	31

DECEMBER 2022

SUNDAY	MONDAY	TUESDAY	WEDNESDAY
27	28	29	30
4	5	6	7 *Full Moon* ○
11	12	13	14
18	19	20	21
25 *Christmas Day*	26 *Kwanzaa, Boxing Day* (CAN)	27 *Christmas Day* *(substitute day, UK)*	28

DECEMBER 2022

THURSDAY	FRIDAY	SATURDAY
	2	3
	9	10
	16	17
	Last Quarter Moon ◑	
	23	24
	New Moon ●	
	30	31
First Quarter Moon ◑		

MONDAY 5

TUESDAY 6

WEDNESDAY 7

Full Moon ○

Let other pens dwell on guilt and misery. I quit such odious subjects
as soon as I can, impatient to restore everybody . . .
to tolerable comfort.

~Mansfield Park (1814)

Thursday 8

Friday 9

Saturday 10

Sunday 11

November 2022

S	M	T	W	T	F	S
		1	2	3	4	5
6	7	8	9	10	11	12
13	14	15	16	17	18	19
20	21	22	23	24	25	26
27	28	29	30			

December 2022

S	M	T	W	T	F	S
				1	2	3
4	5	6	7	8	9	10
11	12	13	14	15	16	17
18	19	20	21	22	23	24
25	26	27	28	29	30	31

January 2023

S	M	T	W	T	F	S
1	2	3	4	5	6	7
8	9	10	11	12	13	14
15	16	17	18	19	20	21
22	23	24	25	26	27	28
29	30	31				

Monday 12

Tuesday 13

Wednesday 14

I do not want people to be very agreeable, as it saves me the trouble of liking them a great deal.

~Letter to Cassandra, December 12, 1798, from *Letters of Jane Austen* (1884)

Thursday 15

Friday 16

Last Quarter Moon ◑

Saturday 17

Sunday 18

November 2022

S	M	T	W	T	F	S
		1	2	3	4	5
6	7	8	9	10	11	12
13	14	15	16	17	18	19
20	21	22	23	24	25	26
27	28	29	30			

December 2022

S	M	T	W	T	F	S
				1	2	3
4	5	6	7	8	9	10
11	12	13	14	15	16	17
18	19	20	21	22	23	24
25	26	27	28	29	30	31

January 2023

S	M	T	W	T	F	S
1	2	3	4	5	6	7
8	9	10	11	12	13	14
15	16	17	18	19	20	21
22	23	24	25	26	27	28
29	30	31				

Monday 19

Tuesday 20

Wednesday 21

Full Moon ○

At Christmas every body invites their friends about them,
and people think little of even the worst weather.

~Emma (1815)

THURSDAY 22

FRIDAY 23

New Moon ●

SATURDAY 24

SUNDAY 25

Christmas Day

November 2022						
S	M	T	W	T	F	S
		1	2	3	4	5
6	7	8	9	10	11	12
13	14	15	16	17	18	19
20	21	22	23	24	25	26
27	28	29	30			

December 2022						
S	M	T	W	T	F	S
				1	2	3
4	5	6	7	8	9	10
11	12	13	14	15	16	17
18	19	20	21	22	23	24
25	26	27	28	29	30	31

January 2023						
S	M	T	W	T	F	S
1	2	3	4	5	6	7
8	9	10	11	12	13	14
15	16	17	18	19	20	21
22	23	24	25	26	27	28
29	30	31				

MONDAY 26

Kwanzaa, Boxing Day (CAN)

TUESDAY 27

Christmas Day (substitute day, UK)

WEDNESDAY 28

Full Moon ○

I have now attained the true art of letter-writing . . .
to express on paper exactly what one would say
to the same person by word of mouth.

~Letter to Cassandra, January 3, 1801,
from *Letters of Jane Austen* (1884)

Thursday 29

First Quarter Moon ◖

Friday 30

Saturday 31

Sunday 1

New Year's Day

November 2022

S	M	T	W	T	F	S
		1	2	3	4	5
6	7	8	9	10	11	12
13	14	15	16	17	18	19
20	21	22	23	24	25	26
27	28	29	30			

December 2022

S	M	T	W	T	F	S
				1	2	3
4	5	6	7	8	9	10
11	12	13	14	15	16	17
18	19	20	21	22	23	24
25	26	27	28	29	30	31

January 2023

S	M	T	W	T	F	S
1	2	3	4	5	6	7
8	9	10	11	12	13	14
15	16	17	18	19	20	21
22	23	24	25	26	27	28
29	30	31				

JANUARY 2023

SUNDAY	MONDAY	TUESDAY	WEDNESDAY
1 *New Year's Day*	2 *Bank holiday (UK, CAN)*	3	4
8	9	10	11
15	16 *Martin Luther King Jr. Day*	17	18
22 *Lunar New Year (Year of the Rabbit)*	23	24	25
29	30	31	1

JANUARY 2023

THURSDAY	FRIDAY	SATURDAY
	6 *Full Moon* ○	**7**
2	**13**	**14** *Last Quarter Moon* ◑
9	**20**	**21** *New Moon* ●
6 *Australia Day*	**27**	**28** *First Quarter Moon* ◑
	3	4

MONDAY 2

Bank holiday (UK, CAN)

TUESDAY 3

WEDNESDAY 4

When you receive this, our guests will be all gone or going; and I shall be left to the comfortable disposal of my time.

~Letter to Cassandra, January 7, 1807,
from *Letters of Jane Austen* (1884)

JANUARY 2023

Thursday 5

Friday 6

Full Moon ○

Saturday 7

Sunday 8

December 2022

S	M	T	W	T	F	S
				1	2	3
4	5	6	7	8	9	10
11	12	13	14	15	16	17
18	19	20	21	22	23	24
25	26	27	28	29	30	31

January 2023

S	M	T	W	T	F	S
1	2	3	4	5	6	7
8	9	10	11	12	13	14
15	16	17	18	19	20	21
22	23	24	25	26	27	28
29	30	31				

February 2023

S	M	T	W	T	F	S
			1	2	3	4
5	6	7	8	9	10	11
12	13	14	15	16	17	18
19	20	21	22	23	24	25
26	27	28				

Monday 9

Tuesday 10

Wednesday 11

Full Moon ○

My idea of good company . . . is the company of clever, well-informed people, who have a great deal of conversation.

~*Persuasion* (1817)

Thursday 12

Friday 13

Saturday 14

Last Quarter Moon ☽

Sunday 15

December 2022

S	M	T	W	T	F	S
				1	2	3
4	5	6	7	8	9	10
11	12	13	14	15	16	17
18	19	20	21	22	23	24
25	26	27	28	29	30	31

January 2023

S	M	T	W	T	F	S
1	2	3	4	5	6	7
8	9	10	11	12	13	14
15	16	17	18	19	20	21
22	23	24	25	26	27	28
29	30	31				

February 2023

S	M	T	W	T	F	S
			1	2	3	4
5	6	7	8	9	10	11
12	13	14	15	16	17	18
19	20	21	22	23	24	25
26	27	28				

MONDAY 16

Martin Luther King Jr. Day

TUESDAY 17

WEDNESDAY 18

Full Moon ○

I am very strong. Nothing ever fatigues me
but doing what I do not like.

~*Mansfield Park* (1814)

THURSDAY 19

FRIDAY 20

SATURDAY 21

New Moon ●

SUNDAY 22

Lunar New Year (Year of the Rabbit)

December 2022						
S	M	T	W	T	F	S
				1	2	3
4	5	6	7	8	9	10
11	12	13	14	15	16	17
18	19	20	21	22	23	24
25	26	27	28	29	30	31

January 2023						
S	M	T	W	T	F	S
1	2	3	4	5	6	7
8	9	10	11	12	13	14
15	16	17	18	19	20	21
22	23	24	25	26	27	28
29	30	31				

February 2023						
S	M	T	W	T	F	S
			1	2	3	4
5	6	7	8	9	10	11
12	13	14	15	16	17	18
19	20	21	22	23	24	25
26	27	28				

MONDAY 23

TUESDAY 24

WEDNESDAY 25

Full Moon ○

Could my ideas flow as fast as the rain in the store-closet
it would be charming.

~Letter to Cassandra, January 24, 1809,
from *Letters of Jane Austen* (1884)

JANUARY 2023

Thursday 26

Australia Day

Friday 27

Saturday 28

First Quarter Moon ◐

Sunday 29

<table>
<tr><td colspan="7" align="center">December 2022</td></tr>
<tr><td>S</td><td>M</td><td>T</td><td>W</td><td>T</td><td>F</td><td>S</td></tr>
<tr><td></td><td></td><td></td><td></td><td>1</td><td>2</td><td>3</td></tr>
<tr><td>4</td><td>5</td><td>6</td><td>7</td><td>8</td><td>9</td><td>10</td></tr>
<tr><td>11</td><td>12</td><td>13</td><td>14</td><td>15</td><td>16</td><td>17</td></tr>
<tr><td>18</td><td>19</td><td>20</td><td>21</td><td>22</td><td>23</td><td>24</td></tr>
<tr><td>25</td><td>26</td><td>27</td><td>28</td><td>29</td><td>30</td><td>31</td></tr>
</table>

<table>
<tr><td colspan="7" align="center">January 2023</td></tr>
<tr><td>S</td><td>M</td><td>T</td><td>W</td><td>T</td><td>F</td><td>S</td></tr>
<tr><td>1</td><td>2</td><td>3</td><td>4</td><td>5</td><td>6</td><td>7</td></tr>
<tr><td>8</td><td>9</td><td>10</td><td>11</td><td>12</td><td>13</td><td>14</td></tr>
<tr><td>15</td><td>16</td><td>17</td><td>18</td><td>19</td><td>20</td><td>21</td></tr>
<tr><td>22</td><td>23</td><td>24</td><td>25</td><td>26</td><td>27</td><td>28</td></tr>
<tr><td>29</td><td>30</td><td>31</td><td></td><td></td><td></td><td></td></tr>
</table>

<table>
<tr><td colspan="7" align="center">February 2023</td></tr>
<tr><td>S</td><td>M</td><td>T</td><td>W</td><td>T</td><td>F</td><td>S</td></tr>
<tr><td></td><td></td><td></td><td>1</td><td>2</td><td>3</td><td>4</td></tr>
<tr><td>5</td><td>6</td><td>7</td><td>8</td><td>9</td><td>10</td><td>11</td></tr>
<tr><td>12</td><td>13</td><td>14</td><td>15</td><td>16</td><td>17</td><td>18</td></tr>
<tr><td>19</td><td>20</td><td>21</td><td>22</td><td>23</td><td>24</td><td>25</td></tr>
<tr><td>26</td><td>27</td><td>28</td><td></td><td></td><td></td><td></td></tr>
</table>

Monday 30

Tuesday 31

Wednesday 1

would recommend to her and Mr. D. the simple regimen of separate rooms.

~Letter to Fanny Knight, February 2, 1817, on Mrs. Deedes having an eighteenth child

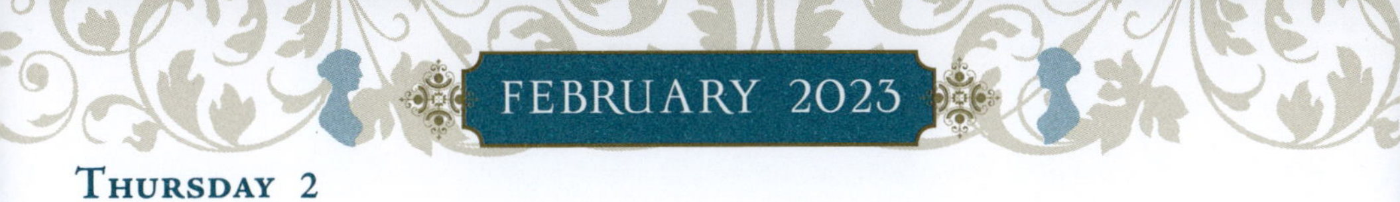

Thursday 2

Groundhog Day

Friday 3

Saturday 4

Sunday 5

Full Moon ○

December 2022						
S	M	T	W	T	F	S
				1	2	3
4	5	6	7	8	9	10
11	12	13	14	15	16	17
18	19	20	21	22	23	24
25	26	27	28	29	30	31

January 2023						
S	M	T	W	T	F	S
1	2	3	4	5	6	7
8	9	10	11	12	13	14
15	16	17	18	19	20	21
22	23	24	25	26	27	28
29	30	31				

February 2023						
S	M	T	W	T	F	S
			1	2	3	4
5	6	7	8	9	10	11
12	13	14	15	16	17	18
19	20	21	22	23	24	25
26	27	28				

FEBRUARY 2023

SUNDAY	MONDAY	TUESDAY	WEDNESDAY
29	30	31	1
5 *Full Moon* ○	6	7	8
12	13 *Last Quarter Moon* ◑	14 *Valentine's Day*	15
19	20 *Presidents' Day* *New Moon* ●	21	22 *Ash Wednesday*
26	27 *First Quarter Moon* ◐	28	1

FEBRUARY 2023

THURSDAY | FRIDAY | SATURDAY

3
4
Groundhog Day
10
11
17
18
24
25
3
4

NOTES

MONDAY 6

TUESDAY 7

WEDNESDAY 8

Full Moon ○

He is so very much occupied by the idea of not being in love
with her, that I should not wonder if it were to
end in his being so at last.

~Emma (1815)

THURSDAY 9

FRIDAY 10

SATURDAY 11

SUNDAY 12

January 2023

S	M	T	W	T	F	S
1	2	3	4	5	6	7
8	9	10	11	12	13	14
15	16	17	18	19	20	21
22	23	24	25	26	27	28
29	30	31				

February 2023

S	M	T	W	T	F	S
			1	2	3	4
5	6	7	8	9	10	11
12	13	14	15	16	17	18
19	20	21	22	23	24	25
26	27	28				

March 2023

S	M	T	W	T	F	S
			1	2	3	4
5	6	7	8	9	10	11
12	13	14	15	16	17	18
19	20	21	22	23	24	25
26	27	28	29	30	31	

MONDAY 13

Last Quarter Moon ◑

TUESDAY 14

Valentine's Day

WEDNESDAY 15

My feelings will not be repressed. You must allow me to tell you how ardently I admire and love you.

~Pride and Prejudice (1813)

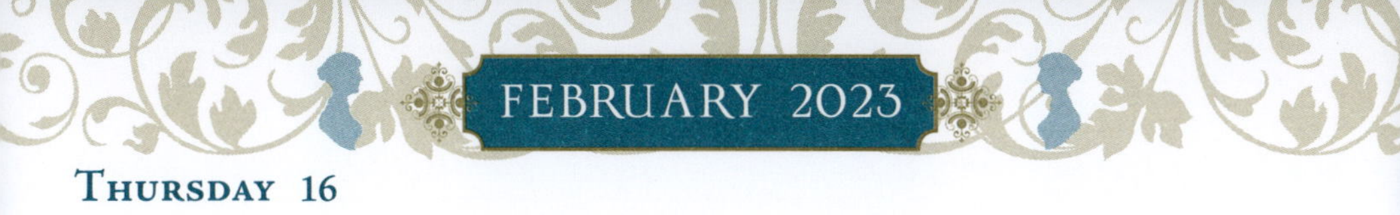

FEBRUARY 2023

Thursday 16

Friday 17

Saturday 18

Sunday 19

January 2023						
S	M	T	W	T	F	S
1	2	3	4	5	6	7
8	9	10	11	12	13	14
15	16	17	18	19	20	21
22	23	24	25	26	27	28
29	30	31				

February 2023						
S	M	T	W	T	F	S
			1	2	3	4
5	6	7	8	9	10	11
12	13	14	15	16	17	18
19	20	21	22	23	24	25
26	27	28				

March 2023						
S	M	T	W	T	F	S
			1	2	3	4
5	6	7	8	9	10	11
12	13	14	15	16	17	18
19	20	21	22	23	24	25
26	27	28	29	30	31	

MONDAY 20

Presidents' Day   *New Moon* ○

TUESDAY 21

WEDNESDAY 22

Ash Wednesday

I come here with no expectations, only to profess,
now that I am at liberty to do so,
that my heart is and always will be . . . yours.

~Sense and Sensibility (1811)

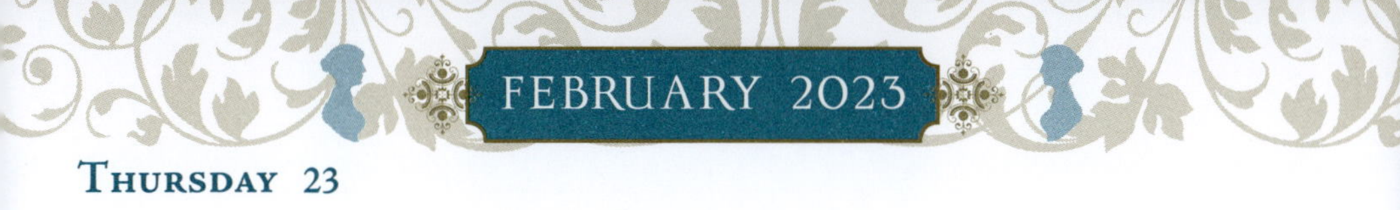

FEBRUARY 2023

Thursday 23

Friday 24

Saturday 25

Sunday 26

January 2023						
S	M	T	W	T	F	S
1	2	3	4	5	6	7
8	9	10	11	12	13	14
15	16	17	18	19	20	21
22	23	24	25	26	27	28
29	30	31				

February 2023						
S	M	T	W	T	F	S
			1	2	3	4
5	6	7	8	9	10	11
12	13	14	15	16	17	18
19	20	21	22	23	24	25
26	27	28				

March 2023						
S	M	T	W	T	F	S
			1	2	3	4
5	6	7	8	9	10	11
12	13	14	15	16	17	18
19	20	21	22	23	24	25
26	27	28	29	30	31	

Monday 27

First Quarter Moon ◑

Tuesday 28

Wednesday 1

Full Moon ○

Before he had been at Mansfield a week, she was quite ready to be fallen in love with.

~*Mansfield Park* (1814)

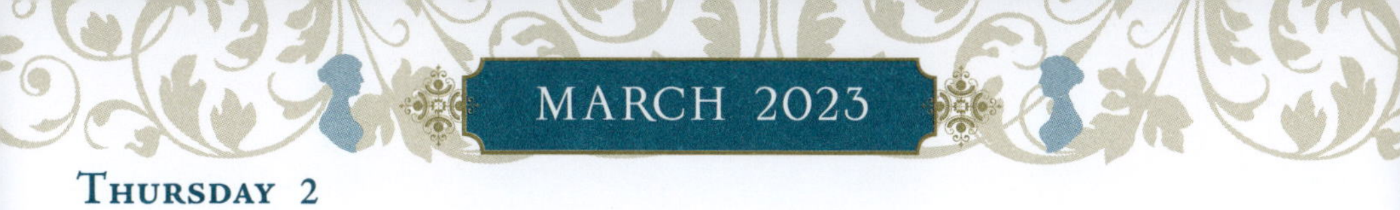

Thursday 2

Friday 3

Saturday 4

Sunday 5

January 2023

S	M	T	W	T	F	S
1	2	3	4	5	6	7
8	9	10	11	12	13	14
15	16	17	18	19	20	21
22	23	24	25	26	27	28
29	30	31				

February 2023

S	M	T	W	T	F	S
			1	2	3	4
5	6	7	8	9	10	11
12	13	14	15	16	17	18
19	20	21	22	23	24	25
26	27	28				

March 2023

S	M	T	W	T	F	S
			1	2	3	4
5	6	7	8	9	10	11
12	13	14	15	16	17	18
19	20	21	22	23	24	25
26	27	28	29	30	31	

MARCH 2023

SUNDAY	MONDAY	TUESDAY	WEDNESDAY
26	27	28	1
5	6	7 *Full Moon* ○	8
12 *Daylight Saving Time Begins (US, CAN)*	13 *Commonwealth Day (UK, CAN, AUS, NZ)*	14 *Last Quarter Moon* ◑	15
19	20	21 *New Moon* ●	22 *Ramadan (begins at sundown)*
26	27	28 *First Quarter Moon* ◐	29

THURSDAY	FRIDAY	SATURDAY
	3	4
	10	11
	17 *St. Patrick's Day*	18
	24	25
	31	1

NOTES

Monday 6

Tuesday 7

Full Moon ○

Wednesday 8

Why did we wait for any thing?—why not seize the pleasure
at once?—How often is happiness destroyed
by preparation, foolish preparation!

~Emma (1815)

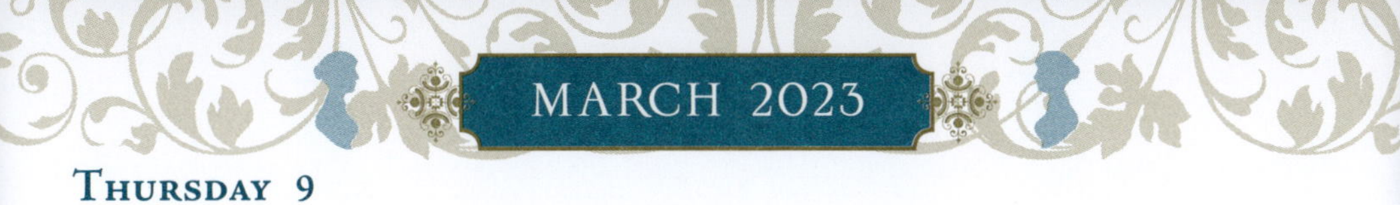

Thursday 9

Friday 10

Saturday 11

Sunday 12

Daylight Saving Time Begins (US, CAN)

February 2023

S	M	T	W	T	F	S
			1	2	3	4
5	6	7	8	9	10	11
12	13	14	15	16	17	18
19	20	21	22	23	24	25
26	27	28				

March 2023

S	M	T	W	T	F	S
			1	2	3	4
5	6	7	8	9	10	11
12	13	14	15	16	17	18
19	20	21	22	23	24	25
26	27	28	29	30	31	

April 2023

S	M	T	W	T	F	S
						1
2	3	4	5	6	7	8
9	10	11	12	13	14	15
16	17	18	19	20	21	22
23	24	25	26	27	28	29
30						

MONDAY 13

Commonwealth Day (UK, CAN, AUS, NZ)

TUESDAY 14

Last Quarter Moon ◑

WEDNESDAY 15

Full Moon ○

There is a quickness of perception in some, a nicety in the discernment of character, a natural penetration . . . which no experience in others can equal.

~*Persuasion* (1817)

MARCH 2023

THURSDAY 16

FRIDAY 17

St. Patrick's Day

SATURDAY 18

SUNDAY 19

February 2023

S	M	T	W	T	F	S
			1	2	3	4
5	6	7	8	9	10	11
12	13	14	15	16	17	18
19	20	21	22	23	24	25
26	27	28				

March 2023

S	M	T	W	T	F	S
			1	2	3	4
5	6	7	8	9	10	11
12	13	14	15	16	17	18
19	20	21	22	23	24	25
26	27	28	29	30	31	

April 2023

S	M	T	W	T	F	S
						1
2	3	4	5	6	7	8
9	10	11	12	13	14	15
16	17	18	19	20	21	22
23	24	25	26	27	28	29
30						

Monday 20

Tuesday 21

New Moon ●

Wednesday 22

Ramadan (begins at sundown)   *Full Moon* ○

What can any body's native air do for them in . . . January,
February, and March? Good fires and carriages
would be much more to the purpose.

~*Emma* (1815)

Thursday 23

Friday 24

Saturday 25

Sunday 26

February 2023

S	M	T	W	T	F	S
			1	2	3	4
5	6	7	8	9	10	11
12	13	14	15	16	17	18
19	20	21	22	23	24	25
26	27	28				

March 2023

S	M	T	W	T	F	S
			1	2	3	4
5	6	7	8	9	10	11
12	13	14	15	16	17	18
19	20	21	22	23	24	25
26	27	28	29	30	31	

April 2023

S	M	T	W	T	F	S
						1
2	3	4	5	6	7	8
9	10	11	12	13	14	15
16	17	18	19	20	21	22
23	24	25	26	27	28	29
30						

Monday 27

Tuesday 28

First Quarter Moon ◗

Wednesday 29

Full Moon ○

I could not sit seriously down to write a serious romance under any other motive than to save my life.

~Letter to Mr. Clarke, April 1, 1816,
from *Letters of Jane Austen* (1884)

Thursday 30

Friday 31

Saturday 1

Sunday 2

Palm Sunday

February 2023

S	M	T	W	T	F	S
			1	2	3	4
5	6	7	8	9	10	11
12	13	14	15	16	17	18
19	20	21	22	23	24	25
26	27	28				

March 2023

S	M	T	W	T	F	S
			1	2	3	4
5	6	7	8	9	10	11
12	13	14	15	16	17	18
19	20	21	22	23	24	25
26	27	28	29	30	31	

April 2023

S	M	T	W	T	F	S
						1
2	3	4	5	6	7	8
9	10	11	12	13	14	15
16	17	18	19	20	21	22
23	24	25	26	27	28	29
30						

APRIL 2023

SUNDAY	MONDAY	TUESDAY	WEDNESDAY
26	27	28	29
2 *Palm Sunday*	3	4	5 *Passover (begins at sundown)*
9 *Easter Sunday*	10 *Easter Monday, Bank holiday (UK)*	11	12
16 *Orthodox Easter*	17	18	19
23 30	24	25 *Anzac Day (AUS, NZ)*	26

APRIL 2023

THURSDAY	FRIDAY	SATURDAY
	31	1
	7	8
Full Moon ○	*Good Friday*	
	14	15
Last Quarter Moon ◑		
	21	22
New Moon ●	*Eid al-Fitr* *(begins at sundown)*	*Earth Day*
	28	29
First Quarter Moon ◑		

NOTES

MONDAY 3

TUESDAY 4

WEDNESDAY 5

Passover (begins at sundown)

Know your own happiness. You want nothing but patience— or give it a more fascinating name, call it hope.

~Sense and Sensibility (1811)

APRIL 2023

Thursday 6

Full Moon ○

Friday 7

Good Friday

Saturday 8

Sunday 9

Easter Sunday

March 2023

S	M	T	W	T	F	S
			1	2	3	4
5	6	7	8	9	10	11
12	13	14	15	16	17	18
19	20	21	22	23	24	25
26	27	28	29	30	31	

April 2023

S	M	T	W	T	F	S
						1
2	3	4	5	6	7	8
9	10	11	12	13	14	15
16	17	18	19	20	21	22
23	24	25	26	27	28	29
30						

May 2023

S	M	T	W	T	F	S
	1	2	3	4	5	6
7	8	9	10	11	12	13
14	15	16	17	18	19	20
21	22	23	24	25	26	27
28	29	30	31			

Monday 10

Easter Monday, Bank holiday (UK)

Tuesday 11

Wednesday 12

Full Moon ○

There is no charm equal to tenderness of heart. . . .
There is nothing to be compared to it.

~Emma (1815)

Thursday 13

Third Quarter Moon ◑

Friday 14

Saturday 15

Sunday 16

Orthodox Easter

March 2023						
S	M	T	W	T	F	S
			1	2	3	4
5	6	7	8	9	10	11
12	13	14	15	16	17	18
19	20	21	22	23	24	25
26	27	28	29	30	31	

April 2023						
S	M	T	W	T	F	S
						1
2	3	4	5	6	7	8
9	10	11	12	13	14	15
16	17	18	19	20	21	22
23	24	25	26	27	28	29
30						

May 2023						
S	M	T	W	T	F	S
	1	2	3	4	5	6
7	8	9	10	11	12	13
14	15	16	17	18	19	20
21	22	23	24	25	26	27
28	29	30	31			

Monday 17

Tuesday 18

Wednesday 19

Full Moon ○

They are much to be pitied who have not . . . at least, been given a taste for Nature in early life. They lose a great deal.

~*Mansfield Park* (1814)

APRIL 2023

THURSDAY 20

New Moon ●

FRIDAY 21

Eid al-Fitr (begins at sundown)

SATURDAY 22

Earth Day

SUNDAY 23

<table>
<tr><td colspan="7">March 2023</td></tr>
<tr><td>S</td><td>M</td><td>T</td><td>W</td><td>T</td><td>F</td><td>S</td></tr>
<tr><td></td><td></td><td></td><td>1</td><td>2</td><td>3</td><td>4</td></tr>
<tr><td>5</td><td>6</td><td>7</td><td>8</td><td>9</td><td>10</td><td>11</td></tr>
<tr><td>12</td><td>13</td><td>14</td><td>15</td><td>16</td><td>17</td><td>18</td></tr>
<tr><td>19</td><td>20</td><td>21</td><td>22</td><td>23</td><td>24</td><td>25</td></tr>
<tr><td>26</td><td>27</td><td>28</td><td>29</td><td>30</td><td>31</td><td></td></tr>
</table>

<table>
<tr><td colspan="7">April 2023</td></tr>
<tr><td>S</td><td>M</td><td>T</td><td>W</td><td>T</td><td>F</td><td>S</td></tr>
<tr><td></td><td></td><td></td><td></td><td></td><td></td><td>1</td></tr>
<tr><td>2</td><td>3</td><td>4</td><td>5</td><td>6</td><td>7</td><td>8</td></tr>
<tr><td>9</td><td>10</td><td>11</td><td>12</td><td>13</td><td>14</td><td>15</td></tr>
<tr><td>16</td><td>17</td><td>18</td><td>19</td><td>20</td><td>21</td><td>22</td></tr>
<tr><td>23</td><td>24</td><td>25</td><td>26</td><td>27</td><td>28</td><td>29</td></tr>
<tr><td>30</td><td></td><td></td><td></td><td></td><td></td><td></td></tr>
</table>

<table>
<tr><td colspan="7">May 2023</td></tr>
<tr><td>S</td><td>M</td><td>T</td><td>W</td><td>T</td><td>F</td><td>S</td></tr>
<tr><td></td><td>1</td><td>2</td><td>3</td><td>4</td><td>5</td><td>6</td></tr>
<tr><td>7</td><td>8</td><td>9</td><td>10</td><td>11</td><td>12</td><td>13</td></tr>
<tr><td>14</td><td>15</td><td>16</td><td>17</td><td>18</td><td>19</td><td>20</td></tr>
<tr><td>21</td><td>22</td><td>23</td><td>24</td><td>25</td><td>26</td><td>27</td></tr>
<tr><td>28</td><td>29</td><td>30</td><td>31</td><td></td><td></td><td></td></tr>
</table>

MONDAY 24

TUESDAY 25

Anzac Day (AUS, NZ)

WEDNESDAY 26

Full Moon ○

Your lilacs are in leaf, ours are in bloom. The horse-chestnuts are quite out, and the elms almost. . . . Everything was fresh and beautiful.

~Letter to Cassandra, April 25 1809, from *Letters of Jane Austen* (1884)

Thursday 27

First Quarter Moon ◐

Friday 28

Saturday 29

Sunday 30

March 2023

S	M	T	W	T	F	S
			1	2	3	4
5	6	7	8	9	10	11
12	13	14	15	16	17	18
19	20	21	22	23	24	25
26	27	28	29	30	31	

April 2023

S	M	T	W	T	F	S
						1
2	3	4	5	6	7	8
9	10	11	12	13	14	15
16	17	18	19	20	21	22
23	24	25	26	27	28	29
30						

May 2023

S	M	T	W	T	F	S
	1	2	3	4	5	6
7	8	9	10	11	12	13
14	15	16	17	18	19	20
21	22	23	24	25	26	27
28	29	30	31			

SUNDAY	MONDAY	TUESDAY	WEDNESDAY
30	1 *May Day (bank holiday UK, IRL)*	2	3
7	8	9	10
14 *Mother's Day*	15	16	17
21	22 *Victoria Day (CAN)*	23	24
28	29 *Memorial Day (US), Spring bank holiday (UK)*	30	31

THURSDAY	FRIDAY	SATURDAY
	5	**6**
	Cinco de Mayo *Full Moon* ○	
	12	**13**
	Last Quarter Moon ◐	
	19	**20**
	New Moon ●	
	26	**27**
		First Quarter Moon ◑
	2	**3**

NOTES

MAY 2023

Monday 1

May Day (bank holiday UK, IRL)

Tuesday 2

Wednesday 3

To sit in the shade on a fine day, and look upon verdure,
is the most perfect refreshment.

~Mansfield Park (1814)

Thursday 4

Friday 5

Cinco de Mayo   *Full Moon* ○

Saturday 6

Sunday 7

April 2023						
S	M	T	W	T	F	S
						1
2	3	4	5	6	7	8
9	10	11	12	13	14	15
16	17	18	19	20	21	22
23	24	25	26	27	28	29
30						

May 2023						
S	M	T	W	T	F	S
	1	2	3	4	5	6
7	8	9	10	11	12	13
14	15	16	17	18	19	20
21	22	23	24	25	26	27
28	29	30	31			

June 2023						
S	M	T	W	T	F	S
				1	2	3
4	5	6	7	8	9	10
11	12	13	14	15	16	17
18	19	20	21	22	23	24
25	26	27	28	29	30	

Monday 8

Tuesday 9

Wednesday 10

Full Moon ○

Well, here we are at Bath. . . . Mother does not seem at all the worse for her journey, nor are any of us, I hope.

~Letter to Cassandra, May 17, 1799, from *Letters of Jane Austen* (1884)

Thursday 11

Friday 12

Last Quarter Moon ◑

Saturday 13

Sunday 14

Mother's Day

<table>
<tr><td colspan="7">April 2023</td></tr>
<tr><td>S</td><td>M</td><td>T</td><td>W</td><td>T</td><td>F</td><td>S</td></tr>
<tr><td></td><td></td><td></td><td></td><td></td><td></td><td>1</td></tr>
<tr><td>2</td><td>3</td><td>4</td><td>5</td><td>6</td><td>7</td><td>8</td></tr>
<tr><td>9</td><td>10</td><td>11</td><td>12</td><td>13</td><td>14</td><td>15</td></tr>
<tr><td>16</td><td>17</td><td>18</td><td>19</td><td>20</td><td>21</td><td>22</td></tr>
<tr><td>23</td><td>24</td><td>25</td><td>26</td><td>27</td><td>28</td><td>29</td></tr>
<tr><td>30</td><td></td><td></td><td></td><td></td><td></td><td></td></tr>
</table>

<table>
<tr><td colspan="7">May 2023</td></tr>
<tr><td>S</td><td>M</td><td>T</td><td>W</td><td>T</td><td>F</td><td>S</td></tr>
<tr><td></td><td>1</td><td>2</td><td>3</td><td>4</td><td>5</td><td>6</td></tr>
<tr><td>7</td><td>8</td><td>9</td><td>10</td><td>11</td><td>12</td><td>13</td></tr>
<tr><td>14</td><td>15</td><td>16</td><td>17</td><td>18</td><td>19</td><td>20</td></tr>
<tr><td>21</td><td>22</td><td>23</td><td>24</td><td>25</td><td>26</td><td>27</td></tr>
<tr><td>28</td><td>29</td><td>30</td><td>31</td><td></td><td></td><td></td></tr>
</table>

<table>
<tr><td colspan="7">June 2023</td></tr>
<tr><td>S</td><td>M</td><td>T</td><td>W</td><td>T</td><td>F</td><td>S</td></tr>
<tr><td></td><td></td><td></td><td></td><td>1</td><td>2</td><td>3</td></tr>
<tr><td>4</td><td>5</td><td>6</td><td>7</td><td>8</td><td>9</td><td>10</td></tr>
<tr><td>11</td><td>12</td><td>13</td><td>14</td><td>15</td><td>16</td><td>17</td></tr>
<tr><td>18</td><td>19</td><td>20</td><td>21</td><td>22</td><td>23</td><td>24</td></tr>
<tr><td>25</td><td>26</td><td>27</td><td>28</td><td>29</td><td>30</td><td></td></tr>
</table>

Monday 15

Tuesday 16

Wednesday 17

Full Moon ○

We are to have a tiny party here tonight. I hate tiny parties, they force one into constant exertion.

~Letter to Cassandra, May 21, 1801, from *Letters of Jane Austen* (1884)

Thursday 18

Friday 19

New Moon ●

Saturday 20

Sunday 21

April 2023						
S	M	T	W	T	F	S
						1
2	3	4	5	6	7	8
9	10	11	12	13	14	15
16	17	18	19	20	21	22
23	24	25	26	27	28	29
30						

May 2023						
S	M	T	W	T	F	S
	1	2	3	4	5	6
7	8	9	10	11	12	13
14	15	16	17	18	19	20
21	22	23	24	25	26	27
28	29	30	31			

June 2023						
S	M	T	W	T	F	S
				1	2	3
4	5	6	7	8	9	10
11	12	13	14	15	16	17
18	19	20	21	22	23	24
25	26	27	28	29	30	

MONDAY 22

Victoria Day (CAN)

TUESDAY 23

WEDNESDAY 24

Full Moon ○

*Selfishness must always be forgiven you know,
because there is no hope of a cure.*

~Mansfield Park (1814)

Thursday 25

Friday 26

Saturday 27

First Quarter Moon ◑

Sunday 28

April 2023						
S	M	T	W	T	F	S
						1
2	3	4	5	6	7	8
9	10	11	12	13	14	15
16	17	18	19	20	21	22
23	24	25	26	27	28	29
30						

May 2023						
S	M	T	W	T	F	S
	1	2	3	4	5	6
7	8	9	10	11	12	13
14	15	16	17	18	19	20
21	22	23	24	25	26	27
28	29	30	31			

June 2023						
S	M	T	W	T	F	S
				1	2	3
4	5	6	7	8	9	10
11	12	13	14	15	16	17
18	19	20	21	22	23	24
25	26	27	28	29	30	

MONDAY 29

Memorial Day (US), Spring bank holiday (UK)

TUESDAY 30

WEDNESDAY 31

I declare after all there is no enjoyment like reading! How much sooner one tires of any thing than of a book!

~*Pride and Prejudice* (1813)

THURSDAY 1

FRIDAY 2

SATURDAY 3

Full Moon ○

SUNDAY 4

April 2023

S	M	T	W	T	F	S
						1
2	3	4	5	6	7	8
9	10	11	12	13	14	15
16	17	18	19	20	21	22
23	24	25	26	27	28	29
30						

May 2023

S	M	T	W	T	F	S
	1	2	3	4	5	6
7	8	9	10	11	12	13
14	15	16	17	18	19	20
21	22	23	24	25	26	27
28	29	30	31			

June 2023

S	M	T	W	T	F	S
				1	2	3
4	5	6	7	8	9	10
11	12	13	14	15	16	17
18	19	20	21	22	23	24
25	26	27	28	29	30	

JUNE 2023

SUNDAY	MONDAY	TUESDAY	WEDNESDAY
28	29	30	31
4	5	6	7
11	12	13	14 *Flag Day (US)*
18 *Father's Day* *New Moon* ●	19 *Juneteenth (US)*	20	21
25	26 *First Quarter Moon* ◑	27	28

JUNE 2023

THURSDAY	FRIDAY	SATURDAY
	2	3 *Full Moon* ○
	9	10 *Last Quarter Moon* ◑
	16	17
	23	24
	30	1

MONDAY 5

TUESDAY 6

WEDNESDAY 7

I find many *douceurs* in being a sort of *chaperon*, for I am put on the sofa near the fire and can drink as much wine as I like.

~Letter to Cassandra, June 11, 1813,
from *Letters of Jane Austen* (1884)

JUNE 2023

THURSDAY 8

FRIDAY 9

SATURDAY 10

Last Quarter Moon ◐

SUNDAY 11

May 2023						
S	M	T	W	T	F	S
	1	2	3	4	5	6
7	8	9	10	11	12	13
14	15	16	17	18	19	20
21	22	23	24	25	26	27
28	29	30	31			

June 2023						
S	M	T	W	T	F	S
				1	2	3
4	5	6	7	8	9	10
11	12	13	14	15	16	17
18	19	20	21	22	23	24
25	26	27	28	29	30	

July 2023						
S	M	T	W	T	F	S
						1
2	3	4	5	6	7	8
9	10	11	12	13	14	15
16	17	18	19	20	21	22
23	24	25	26	27	28	29
30	31					

MONDAY 12

TUESDAY 13

WEDNESDAY 14

What an excellent father you have. . . . I do not know how you
will ever make him amends for his kindness;
or me either, for that matter.

~Pride and Prejudice (1813)

THURSDAY 15

FRIDAY 16

SATURDAY 17

SUNDAY 18

Father's Day

New Moon ●

			May 2023			
S	M	T	W	T	F	S
	1	2	3	4	5	6
7	8	9	10	11	12	13
14	15	16	17	18	19	20
21	22	23	24	25	26	27
28	29	30	31			

			June 2023			
S	M	T	W	T	F	S
				1	2	3
4	5	6	7	8	9	10
11	12	13	14	15	16	17
18	19	20	21	22	23	24
25	26	27	28	29	30	

			July 2023			
S	M	T	W	T	F	S
						1
2	3	4	5	6	7	8
9	10	11	12	13	14	15
16	17	18	19	20	21	22
23	24	25	26	27	28	29
30	31					

MONDAY 19

Juneteenth (US)

TUESDAY 20

WEDNESDAY 21

I was deceived—my breakfast supplied only two ideas—
that the rolls were good and the butter bad.

~Letter to Cassandra, June 19, 1799,
from *Letters of Jane Austen* (1884)

JUNE 2023

Thursday 22

Friday 23

Saturday 24

Sunday 25

May 2023

S	M	T	W	T	F	S
	1	2	3	4	5	6
7	8	9	10	11	12	13
14	15	16	17	18	19	20
21	22	23	24	25	26	27
28	29	30	31			

June 2023

S	M	T	W	T	F	S
				1	2	3
4	5	6	7	8	9	10
11	12	13	14	15	16	17
18	19	20	21	22	23	24
25	26	27	28	29	30	

July 2023

S	M	T	W	T	F	S
						1
2	3	4	5	6	7	8
9	10	11	12	13	14	15
16	17	18	19	20	21	22
23	24	25	26	27	28	29
30	31					

MONDAY 26

First Quarter Moon ◑

TUESDAY 27

WEDNESDAY 28

One half of the world cannot understand
the pleasures of the other.

~Emma (1815)

THURSDAY 29

FRIDAY 30

SATURDAY 1

Canada Day

SUNDAY 2

May 2023						
S	M	T	W	T	F	S
	1	2	3	4	5	6
7	8	9	10	11	12	13
14	15	16	17	18	19	20
21	22	23	24	25	26	27
28	29	30	31			

June 2023						
S	M	T	W	T	F	S
				1	2	3
4	5	6	7	8	9	10
11	12	13	14	15	16	17
18	19	20	21	22	23	24
25	26	27	28	29	30	

July 2023						
S	M	T	W	T	F	S
						1
2	3	4	5	6	7	8
9	10	11	12	13	14	15
16	17	18	19	20	21	22
23	24	25	26	27	28	29
30	31					

JULY 2023

SUNDAY	MONDAY	TUESDAY	WEDNESDAY
25	26	27	28
2	3 *Full Moon* ○	4 *Independence Day (US)*	5
9 *Last Quarter Moon* ◑	10	11	12
16	17 *New Moon* ●	18	19
23 30	24 31	25 *First Quarter Moon* ◐	26

THURSDAY	FRIDAY	SATURDAY
9	30	1 *Canada Day (CAN)*
6	7	8
13	14	15
20	21	22
27	28	29

NOTES

Monday 3

Full Moon ○

Tuesday 4

Independence Day (US)

Wednesday 5

I am only resolved to act in that manner, which will, in my own opinion, constitute my happiness.

~Pride and Prejudice (1813)

Thursday 6

Friday 7

Saturday 8

Sunday 9

Last Quarter Moon ◖

June 2023						
S	M	T	W	T	F	S
				1	2	3
4	5	6	7	8	9	10
11	12	13	14	15	16	17
18	19	20	21	22	23	24
25	26	27	28	29	30	

July 2023						
S	M	T	W	T	F	S
						1
2	3	4	5	6	7	8
9	10	11	12	13	14	15
16	17	18	19	20	21	22
23	24	25	26	27	28	29
30	31					

August 2023						
S	M	T	W	T	F	S
		1	2	3	4	5
6	7	8	9	10	11	12
13	14	15	16	17	18	19
20	21	22	23	24	25	26
27	28	29	30	31		

MONDAY 10

TUESDAY 11

WEDNESDAY 12

For six weeks, I allow Bath is pleasant enough; but beyond *that,*
it is the most tiresome place in the world.

~*Northanger Abbey* (1817)

Thursday 13

Friday 14

Saturday 15

Sunday 16

June 2023						
S	M	T	W	T	F	S
				1	2	3
4	5	6	7	8	9	10
11	12	13	14	15	16	17
18	19	20	21	22	23	24
25	26	27	28	29	30	

July 2023						
S	M	T	W	T	F	S
						1
2	3	4	5	6	7	8
9	10	11	12	13	14	15
16	17	18	19	20	21	22
23	24	25	26	27	28	29
30	31					

August 2023						
S	M	T	W	T	F	S
		1	2	3	4	5
6	7	8	9	10	11	12
13	14	15	16	17	18	19
20	21	22	23	24	25	26
27	28	29	30	31		

MONDAY 17

New Moon ●

TUESDAY 18

WEDNESDAY 19

But, my dear papa, it is supposed to be summer;
a warm day in summer. Look at the tree.

~*Emma* (1815)

THURSDAY 20

FRIDAY 21

SATURDAY 22

SUNDAY 23

June 2023						
S	M	T	W	T	F	S
				1	2	3
4	5	6	7	8	9	10
11	12	13	14	15	16	17
18	19	20	21	22	23	24
25	26	27	28	29	30	

July 2023						
S	M	T	W	T	F	S
						1
2	3	4	5	6	7	8
9	10	11	12	13	14	15
16	17	18	19	20	21	22
23	24	25	26	27	28	29
30	31					

August 2023						
S	M	T	W	T	F	S
		1	2	3	4	5
6	7	8	9	10	11	12
13	14	15	16	17	18	19
20	21	22	23	24	25	26
27	28	29	30	31		

MONDAY 24

TUESDAY 25

First Quarter Moon ☽

WEDNESDAY 26

> **T**here is nothing I would not do for those who are really
> my friends. I have no notion of loving people
> by halves, it is not my nature.
>
> ~*Northanger Abbey* (1817)

JULY 2023

THURSDAY 27

FRIDAY 28

Summer bank holiday (UK)

SATURDAY 29

SUNDAY 30

<table>
<tr><td colspan="7">June 2023</td></tr>
<tr><td>S</td><td>M</td><td>T</td><td>W</td><td>T</td><td>F</td><td>S</td></tr>
<tr><td></td><td></td><td></td><td></td><td>1</td><td>2</td><td>3</td></tr>
<tr><td>4</td><td>5</td><td>6</td><td>7</td><td>8</td><td>9</td><td>10</td></tr>
<tr><td>11</td><td>12</td><td>13</td><td>14</td><td>15</td><td>16</td><td>17</td></tr>
<tr><td>18</td><td>19</td><td>20</td><td>21</td><td>22</td><td>23</td><td>24</td></tr>
<tr><td>25</td><td>26</td><td>27</td><td>28</td><td>29</td><td>30</td><td></td></tr>
</table>

<table>
<tr><td colspan="7">July 2023</td></tr>
<tr><td>S</td><td>M</td><td>T</td><td>W</td><td>T</td><td>F</td><td>S</td></tr>
<tr><td></td><td></td><td></td><td></td><td></td><td></td><td>1</td></tr>
<tr><td>2</td><td>3</td><td>4</td><td>5</td><td>6</td><td>7</td><td>8</td></tr>
<tr><td>9</td><td>10</td><td>11</td><td>12</td><td>13</td><td>14</td><td>15</td></tr>
<tr><td>16</td><td>17</td><td>18</td><td>19</td><td>20</td><td>21</td><td>22</td></tr>
<tr><td>23</td><td>24</td><td>25</td><td>26</td><td>27</td><td>28</td><td>29</td></tr>
<tr><td>30</td><td>31</td><td></td><td></td><td></td><td></td><td></td></tr>
</table>

<table>
<tr><td colspan="7">August 2023</td></tr>
<tr><td>S</td><td>M</td><td>T</td><td>W</td><td>T</td><td>F</td><td>S</td></tr>
<tr><td></td><td></td><td>1</td><td>2</td><td>3</td><td>4</td><td>5</td></tr>
<tr><td>6</td><td>7</td><td>8</td><td>9</td><td>10</td><td>11</td><td>12</td></tr>
<tr><td>13</td><td>14</td><td>15</td><td>16</td><td>17</td><td>18</td><td>19</td></tr>
<tr><td>20</td><td>21</td><td>22</td><td>23</td><td>24</td><td>25</td><td>26</td></tr>
<tr><td>27</td><td>28</td><td>29</td><td>30</td><td>31</td><td></td><td></td></tr>
</table>

Monday 31

Tuesday 1

Full Moon ○

Wednesday 2

My business was to declare myself a scoundrel,
and whether I did it with a bow or a
bluster was of little importance.

~*Sense and Sensibility* (1811)

THURSDAY 3

FRIDAY 4

SATURDAY 5

SUNDAY 6

June 2023

S	M	T	W	T	F	S
				1	2	3
4	5	6	7	8	9	10
11	12	13	14	15	16	17
18	19	20	21	22	23	24
25	26	27	28	29	30	

July 2023

S	M	T	W	T	F	S
						1
2	3	4	5	6	7	8
9	10	11	12	13	14	15
16	17	18	19	20	21	22
23	24	25	26	27	28	29
30	31					

August 2023

S	M	T	W	T	F	S
		1	2	3	4	5
6	7	8	9	10	11	12
13	14	15	16	17	18	19
20	21	22	23	24	25	26
27	28	29	30	31		

AUGUST 2023

SUNDAY	MONDAY	TUESDAY	WEDNESDAY
30	31	1 *Full Moon* ○	2
6	7	8 *Last Quarter Moon* ◑	9
13	14	15	16 *New Moon* ●
20	21	22	23
27	28 *Summer bank holiday (UK)*	29	30 *Full Moon* ○

THURSDAY	FRIDAY	SATURDAY
	4	5
	11	12
	18	19
	25	26
First Quarter Moon ◑	1	2

NOTES

MONDAY 7

TUESDAY 8

Last Quarter Moon ◑

WEDNESDAY 9

I am very much obliged to you for sending your MS.
It has entertained me extremely....
The spirit does not droop at all.

~Letter to her niece, Anna, August 1814,
from *Letters of Jane Austen* (1884)

Thursday 10

Friday 11

Saturday 12

Sunday 13

July 2023

S	M	T	W	T	F	S
						1
2	3	4	5	6	7	8
9	10	11	12	13	14	15
16	17	18	19	20	21	22
23	24	25	26	27	28	29
30	31					

August 2023

S	M	T	W	T	F	S
		1	2	3	4	5
6	7	8	9	10	11	12
13	14	15	16	17	18	19
20	21	22	23	24	25	26
27	28	29	30	31		

September 2023

S	M	T	W	T	F	S
					1	2
3	4	5	6	7	8	9
10	11	12	13	14	15	16
17	18	19	20	21	22	23
24	25	26	27	28	29	30

MONDAY 14

TUESDAY 15

WEDNESDAY 16

New Moon ●

Surprises are foolish things. The pleasure is not enhanced,
and the inconvenience is often considerable.

~Emma (1815)

THURSDAY 17

FRIDAY 18

SATURDAY 19

SUNDAY 20

July 2023

S	M	T	W	T	F	S
						1
2	3	4	5	6	7	8
9	10	11	12	13	14	15
16	17	18	19	20	21	22
23	24	25	26	27	28	29
30	31					

August 2023

S	M	T	W	T	F	S
		1	2	3	4	5
6	7	8	9	10	11	12
13	14	15	16	17	18	19
20	21	22	23	24	25	26
27	28	29	30	31		

September 2023

S	M	T	W	T	F	S
					1	2
3	4	5	6	7	8	9
10	11	12	13	14	15	16
17	18	19	20	21	22	23
24	25	26	27	28	29	30

MONDAY 21

TUESDAY 22

WEDNESDAY 23

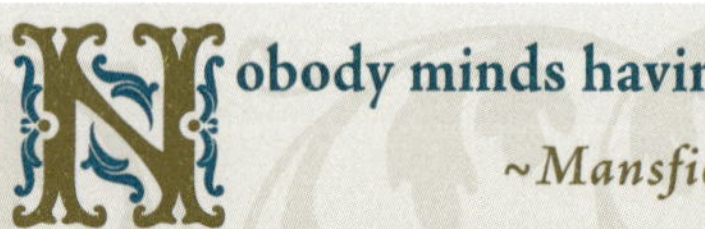

obody minds having what is too good for them.

~Mansfield Park (1814)

Thursday 24

First Quarter Moon ◑

Friday 25

Saturday 26

Sunday 27

July 2023

S	M	T	W	T	F	S
						1
2	3	4	5	6	7	8
9	10	11	12	13	14	15
16	17	18	19	20	21	22
23	24	25	26	27	28	29
30	31					

August 2023

S	M	T	W	T	F	S
		1	2	3	4	5
6	7	8	9	10	11	12
13	14	15	16	17	18	19
20	21	22	23	24	25	26
27	28	29	30	31		

September 2023

S	M	T	W	T	F	S
					1	2
3	4	5	6	7	8	9
10	11	12	13	14	15	16
17	18	19	20	21	22	23
24	25	26	27	28	29	30

MONDAY 28

Summer bank holiday (UK)

TUESDAY 29

WEDNESDAY 30

Full Moon ○

Sometimes one is guided by what they say of themselves,
and very frequently by what other people say of them,
without giving oneself time to deliberate and judge.

~*Sense and Sensibility* (1811)

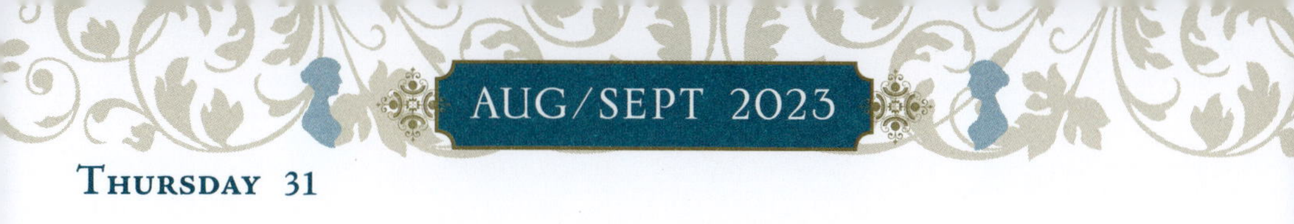

THURSDAY 31

FRIDAY 1

SATURDAY 2

SUNDAY 3

July 2023

S	M	T	W	T	F	S
						1
2	3	4	5	6	7	8
9	10	11	12	13	14	15
16	17	18	19	20	21	22
23	24	25	26	27	28	29
30	31					

August 2023

S	M	T	W	T	F	S
		1	2	3	4	5
6	7	8	9	10	11	12
13	14	15	16	17	18	19
20	21	22	23	24	25	26
27	28	29	30	31		

September 2023

S	M	T	W	T	F	S
					1	2
3	4	5	6	7	8	9
10	11	12	13	14	15	16
17	18	19	20	21	22	23
24	25	26	27	28	29	30

SEPTEMBER 2023

SUNDAY	MONDAY	TUESDAY	WEDNESDAY
27	28	29	30
3	4 *Labor Day (US, CAN)*	5	6 *Last Quarter Moon* ◖
10	11	12	13
17	18	19	20
24 *Yom Kippur* *(begins at sundown)*	25	26	27

SEPTEMBER 2023

THURSDAY	FRIDAY	SATURDAY
	1	2
	8	9
	15	16
ew Moon ●	Rosh Hashanah (begins at sundown)	
	22	23
	First Quarter Moon ◑	
	29	30
	Full Moon ○	

MONDAY 4

Labor Day (US, CAN)

TUESDAY 5

WEDNESDAY 6

Last Quarter Moon ◑

But I believe my feelings are stronger than anybody's;
I am sure they are too strong for my own peace.

~Northanger Abbey (1817)

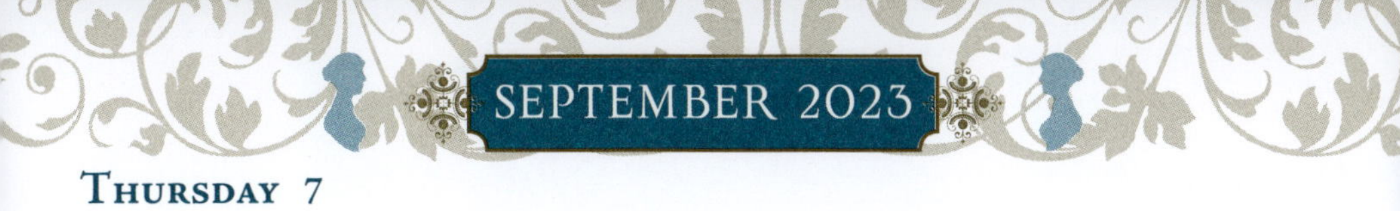

Thursday 7

Friday 8

Saturday 9

Sunday 10

August 2023						
S	M	T	W	T	F	S
		1	2	3	4	5
6	7	8	9	10	11	12
13	14	15	16	17	18	19
20	21	22	23	24	25	26
27	28	29	30	31		

September 2023						
S	M	T	W	T	F	S
					1	2
3	4	5	6	7	8	9
10	11	12	13	14	15	16
17	18	19	20	21	22	23
24	25	26	27	28	29	30

October 202						
S	M	T	W	T	F	S
1	2	3	4	5	6	7
8	9	10	11	12	13	14
15	16	17	18	19	20	21
22	23	24	25	26	27	28
29	30	31				

MONDAY 11

TUESDAY 12

WEDNESDAY 13

You must be the best judge of your own happiness.

~Emma (1815)

THURSDAY 14

New Moon ●

FRIDAY 15

Rosh Hashanah (begins at sundown)

SATURDAY 16

SUNDAY 17

August 2023						
S	M	T	W	T	F	S
		1	2	3	4	5
6	7	8	9	10	11	12
13	14	15	16	17	18	19
20	21	22	23	24	25	26
27	28	29	30	31		

September 2023						
S	M	T	W	T	F	S
					1	2
3	4	5	6	7	8	9
10	11	12	13	14	15	16
17	18	19	20	21	22	23
24	25	26	27	28	29	30

October 202						
S	M	T	W	T	F	S
1	2	3	4	5	6	7
8	9	10	11	12	13	14
15	16	17	18	19	20	21
22	23	24	25	26	27	28
29	30	31				

MONDAY 18

TUESDAY 19

WEDNESDAY 20

I must endeavor to subdue my mind to my fortune. I must learn to brook being happier than I deserve.

~*Persuasion* (1817)

SEPTEMBER 2023

THURSDAY 21

FRIDAY 22

First Quarter Moon ◐

SATURDAY 23

August 2023						
S	M	T	W	T	F	S
		1	2	3	4	5
6	7	8	9	10	11	12
13	14	15	16	17	18	19
20	21	22	23	24	25	26
27	28	29	30	31		

September 2023						
S	M	T	W	T	F	S
					1	2
3	4	5	6	7	8	9
10	11	12	13	14	15	16
17	18	19	20	21	22	23
24	25	26	27	28	29	30

SUNDAY 24

Yom Kippur (begins at sundown)

October 202						
S	M	T	W	T	F	S
1	2	3	4	5	6	7
8	9	10	11	12	13	14
15	16	17	18	19	20	21
22	23	24	25	26	27	28
29	30	31				

Monday 25

Tuesday 26

Wednesday 27

Let me know when you begin the new tea, and the new white wine.... I am still a cat if I see a mouse.

~Letter to Cassandra, September 23, 1813, from *Letters of Jane Austen* (1884)

THURSDAY 28

FRIDAY 29

Full Moon ○

SATURDAY 30

SUNDAY 1

August 2023

S	M	T	W	T	F	S
		1	2	3	4	5
6	7	8	9	10	11	12
13	14	15	16	17	18	19
20	21	22	23	24	25	26
27	28	29	30	31		

September 2023

S	M	T	W	T	F	S
					1	2
3	4	5	6	7	8	9
10	11	12	13	14	15	16
17	18	19	20	21	22	23
24	25	26	27	28	29	30

October 202

S	M	T	W	T	F	S
1	2	3	4	5	6	7
8	9	10	11	12	13	14
15	16	17	18	19	20	21
22	23	24	25	26	27	28
29	30	31				

OCTOBER 2023

SUNDAY	MONDAY	TUESDAY	WEDNESDAY
1	2	3	4
8	9 *Indigenous Peoples' Day, Columbus Day (US), Thanksgiving (CAN)*	10	11
15	16	17	18
22	23	24	25
29	30	31 *Halloween*	1

OCTOBER 2023

THURSDAY	FRIDAY	SATURDAY
	6 *Last Quarter Moon* ◑	7
2	13	14 *New Moon* ●
	20	21 *First Quarter Moon* ◐
	27	28 *Full Moon* ○
	3	4

NOTES

Monday 2

Tuesday 3

Wednesday 4

Her pleasure in the walk must arise from . . . repeating to herself
some few of the thousand poetical descriptions
extant of autumn.

~*Persuasion* (1817)

Thursday 5

Friday 6

Last Quarter Moon ◑

Saturday 7

Sunday 8

September 2023

S	M	T	W	T	F	S
					1	2
3	4	5	6	7	8	9
10	11	12	13	14	15	16
17	18	19	20	21	22	23
24	25	26	27	28	29	30

October 2023

S	M	T	W	T	F	S
1	2	3	4	5	6	7
8	9	10	11	12	13	14
15	16	17	18	19	20	21
22	23	24	25	26	27	28
29	30	31				

November 2023

S	M	T	W	T	F	S
			1	2	3	4
5	6	7	8	9	10	11
12	13	14	15	16	17	18
19	20	21	22	23	24	25
26	27	28	29	30		

Monday 9

Indigenous Peoples' Day, Columbus Day (US), Thanksgiving (CAN)

Tuesday 10

Wednesday 11

cannot attempt to thank you . . . thanks are out of the question.
I feel much more than I can possibly express.

~Mansfield Park (1814)

OCTOBER 2023

THURSDAY 12

FRIDAY 13

SATURDAY 14

New Moon ●

SUNDAY 15

September 2023						
S	M	T	W	T	F	S
					1	2
3	4	5	6	7	8	9
10	11	12	13	14	15	16
17	18	19	20	21	22	23
24	25	26	27	28	29	30

October 2023						
S	M	T	W	T	F	S
1	2	3	4	5	6	7
8	9	10	11	12	13	14
15	16	17	18	19	20	21
22	23	24	25	26	27	28
29	30	31				

November 2023						
S	M	T	W	T	F	S
			1	2	3	4
5	6	7	8	9	10	11
12	13	14	15	16	17	18
19	20	21	22	23	24	25
26	27	28	29	30		

OCTOBER 2023

MONDAY 16

TUESDAY 17

WEDNESDAY 18

Silly things do cease to be silly if they are done by
sensible people in an impudent way.

~Emma (1815)

Thursday 19

Friday 20

Saturday 21

First Quarter Moon ◑

Sunday 22

September 2023						
S	M	T	W	T	F	S
					1	2
3	4	5	6	7	8	9
10	11	12	13	14	15	16
17	18	19	20	21	22	23
24	25	26	27	28	29	30

October 2023						
S	M	T	W	T	F	S
1	2	3	4	5	6	7
8	9	10	11	12	13	14
15	16	17	18	19	20	21
22	23	24	25	26	27	28
29	30	31				

November 2023						
S	M	T	W	T	F	S
			1	2	3	4
5	6	7	8	9	10	11
12	13	14	15	16	17	18
19	20	21	22	23	24	25
26	27	28	29	30		

MONDAY 23

TUESDAY 24

WEDNESDAY 25

It came into my head that at this time of year we have not summer evenings. We shall watch the light to-day.

~Letter to Cassandra, October 24, 1808,
from *Letters of Jane Austen* (1884)

THURSDAY 26

FRIDAY 27

SATURDAY 28

Full Moon ○

SUNDAY 29

September 2023						
S	M	T	W	T	F	S
					1	2
3	4	5	6	7	8	9
10	11	12	13	14	15	16
17	18	19	20	21	22	23
24	25	26	27	28	29	30

October 2023						
S	M	T	W	T	F	S
1	2	3	4	5	6	7
8	9	10	11	12	13	14
15	16	17	18	19	20	21
22	23	24	25	26	27	28
29	30	31				

November 2023						
S	M	T	W	T	F	S
			1	2	3	4
5	6	7	8	9	10	11
12	13	14	15	16	17	18
19	20	21	22	23	24	25
26	27	28	29	30		

Monday 30

Tuesday 31

Halloween

Wednesday 1

Hollow murmurs seemed to creep along the gallery,
and more than once her blood was
chilled by the sound of distant moans.

~Northanger Abbey (1817)

THURSDAY 2

FRIDAY 3

SATURDAY 4

SUNDAY 5

Daylight Saving Time Ends (US, CAN)   *Last Quarter Moon* ◑

September 2023						
S	M	T	W	T	F	S
					1	2
3	4	5	6	7	8	9
10	11	12	13	14	15	16
17	18	19	20	21	22	23
24	25	26	27	28	29	30

October 2023						
S	M	T	W	T	F	S
1	2	3	4	5	6	7
8	9	10	11	12	13	14
15	16	17	18	19	20	21
22	23	24	25	26	27	28
29	30	31				

November 2023						
S	M	T	W	T	F	S
			1	2	3	4
5	6	7	8	9	10	11
12	13	14	15	16	17	18
19	20	21	22	23	24	25
26	27	28	29	30		

NOVEMBER 2023

SUNDAY	MONDAY	TUESDAY	WEDNESDAY
29	30	31	1
5 *Daylight Saving Time Ends (US, CAN)* *Last Quarter Moon* ◑	6	7 *Election Day (US)*	8
12	13 *New Moon* ●	14	15
19	20 *First Quarter Moon* ◐	21	22
26	27 *Full Moon* ○	28	29

THURSDAY	FRIDAY	SATURDAY
	3	4
	10	11 *Veterans Day (US)*
6	17	18
3 *hanksgiving (US)*	24	25
0	1	2

NOTES

MONDAY 6

TUESDAY 7

Election Day (US)

WEDNESDAY 8

Henry suffered the subject to decline . . . he shortly found
himself arrived at politics; and from politics,
it was an easy step to silence.

~*Northanger Abbey* (1817)

THURSDAY 9

FRIDAY 10

SATURDAY 11

Veterans Day (US)

SUNDAY 12

October 2023						
S	M	T	W	T	F	S
1	2	3	4	5	6	7
8	9	10	11	12	13	14
15	16	17	18	19	20	21
22	23	24	25	26	27	28
29	30	31				

November 2023						
S	M	T	W	T	F	S
			1	2	3	4
5	6	7	8	9	10	11
12	13	14	15	16	17	18
19	20	21	22	23	24	25
26	27	28	29	30		

December 2023						
S	M	T	W	T	F	S
					1	2
3	4	5	6	7	8	9
10	11	12	13	14	15	16
17	18	19	20	21	22	23
24	5	26	27	28	29	30
31						

MONDAY 13

New Moon ●

TUESDAY 14

WEDNESDAY 15

I believe I drank too much wine last night at Hurstbourne. . . .
Kindly make allowance therefore for
any indistinctness of writing.

~Letter to Cassandra, November 20, 1800,
from *Letters of Jane Austen*

Thursday 16

Friday 17

Saturday 18

Sunday 19

October 2023

S	M	T	W	T	F	S
1	2	3	4	5	6	7
8	9	10	11	12	13	14
15	16	17	18	19	20	21
22	23	24	25	26	27	28
29	30	31				

November 2023

S	M	T	W	T	F	S
			1	2	3	4
5	6	7	8	9	10	11
12	13	14	15	16	17	18
19	20	21	22	23	24	25
26	27	28	29	30		

December 2023

S	M	T	W	T	F	S
					1	2
3	4	5	6	7	8	9
10	11	12	13	14	15	16
17	18	19	20	21	22	23
24	5	26	27	28	29	30
31						

Monday 20

First Quarter Moon ◐

Tuesday 21

Wednesday 22

Serious she was, very serious in her thankfulness, and in her resolutions; and yet there was no preventing a laugh, sometimes in the very midst of them.

~Emma (1815)

NOVEMBER 2023

Thursday 23

Thanksgiving (US)

Friday 24

Saturday 25

Sunday 26

October 2023						
S	M	T	W	T	F	S
1	2	3	4	5	6	7
8	9	10	11	12	13	14
15	16	17	18	19	20	21
22	23	24	25	26	27	28
29	30	31				

November 2023						
S	M	T	W	T	F	S
			1	2	3	4
5	6	7	8	9	10	11
12	13	14	15	16	17	18
19	20	21	22	23	24	25
26	27	28	29	30		

December 2023						
S	M	T	W	T	F	S
					1	2
3	4	5	6	7	8	9
10	11	12	13	14	15	16
17	18	19	20	21	22	23
24	5	26	27	28	29	30
31						

MONDAY 27

Full Moon ○

TUESDAY 28

WEDNESDAY 29

This exquisite weather is too good. . . . I enjoy it all over me, from top to toe, from right to left, longitudinally, perpendicularly, diagonally.

~Letter to Cassandra, December 2, 1815, from *Letters of Jane Austen* (1884)

THURSDAY 30

FRIDAY 1

SATURDAY 2

SUNDAY 3

October 2023

S	M	T	W	T	F	S
1	2	3	4	5	6	7
8	9	10	11	12	13	14
15	16	17	18	19	20	21
22	23	24	25	26	27	28
29	30	31				

November 2023

S	M	T	W	T	F	S
			1	2	3	4
5	6	7	8	9	10	11
12	13	14	15	16	17	18
19	20	21	22	23	24	25
26	27	28	29	30		

December 2023

S	M	T	W	T	F	S
					1	2
3	4	5	6	7	8	9
10	11	12	13	14	15	16
17	18	19	20	21	22	23
24	5	26	27	28	29	30
31						

DECEMBER 2023

SUNDAY	MONDAY	TUESDAY	WEDNESDAY
26	27	28	29
3	4	5 *Last Quarter Moon* ◑	6
10	11	12 *New Moon* ●	13
17	18	19 *First Quarter Moon* ◐	20
24 **31**	25 *Christmas Day*	26 *Kwanzaa, Boxing Day (CAN)* *Full Moon* ○	27

THURSDAY	FRIDAY	SATURDAY
	1	2
8	9
15	16
22	23
29	30

NOTES

MONDAY 4

TUESDAY 5

Last Quarter Moon ◑

WEDNESDAY 6

And books! . . . she would buy up every copy, I believe,
to prevent their falling into unworthy hands.

~Sense and Sensibility (1811)

DECEMBER 2023

Thursday 7

Friday 8

Saturday 9

Sunday 10

November 2023						
S	M	T	W	T	F	S
			1	2	3	4
5	6	7	8	9	10	11
12	13	14	15	16	17	18
19	20	21	22	23	24	25
26	27	28	29	30		

December 2023						
S	M	T	W	T	F	S
					1	2
3	4	5	6	7	8	9
10	11	12	13	14	15	16
17	18	19	20	21	22	23
24	25	26	27	28	29	30
31						

January 2024						
S	M	T	W	T	F	S
	1	2	3	4	5	6
7	8	9	10	11	12	13
14	15	16	17	18	19	20
21	22	23	24	25	26	27
28	29	30	31			

MONDAY 11

TUESDAY 12

New Moon ●

WEDNESDAY 13

I took the liberty a few days ago of asking your black velvet bonnet to lend me its cawl [back part], which it very readily did.

~Letter to Cassandra, December 18, 1798,
from *Letters of Jane Austen* (1884)

THURSDAY 14

FRIDAY 15

SATURDAY 16

SUNDAY 17

<table>
<tr><td colspan="7">November 2023</td></tr>
<tr><td>S</td><td>M</td><td>T</td><td>W</td><td>T</td><td>F</td><td>S</td></tr>
<tr><td></td><td></td><td></td><td>1</td><td>2</td><td>3</td><td>4</td></tr>
<tr><td>5</td><td>6</td><td>7</td><td>8</td><td>9</td><td>10</td><td>11</td></tr>
<tr><td>12</td><td>13</td><td>14</td><td>15</td><td>16</td><td>17</td><td>18</td></tr>
<tr><td>19</td><td>20</td><td>21</td><td>22</td><td>23</td><td>24</td><td>25</td></tr>
<tr><td>26</td><td>27</td><td>28</td><td>29</td><td>30</td><td></td><td></td></tr>
</table>

<table>
<tr><td colspan="7">December 2023</td></tr>
<tr><td>S</td><td>M</td><td>T</td><td>W</td><td>T</td><td>F</td><td>S</td></tr>
<tr><td></td><td></td><td></td><td></td><td></td><td>1</td><td>2</td></tr>
<tr><td>3</td><td>4</td><td>5</td><td>6</td><td>7</td><td>8</td><td>9</td></tr>
<tr><td>10</td><td>11</td><td>12</td><td>13</td><td>14</td><td>15</td><td>16</td></tr>
<tr><td>17</td><td>18</td><td>19</td><td>20</td><td>21</td><td>22</td><td>23</td></tr>
<tr><td>24</td><td>25</td><td>26</td><td>27</td><td>28</td><td>29</td><td>30</td></tr>
<tr><td>31</td><td></td><td></td><td></td><td></td><td></td><td></td></tr>
</table>

<table>
<tr><td colspan="7">January 2024</td></tr>
<tr><td>S</td><td>M</td><td>T</td><td>W</td><td>T</td><td>F</td><td>S</td></tr>
<tr><td></td><td>1</td><td>2</td><td>3</td><td>4</td><td>5</td><td>6</td></tr>
<tr><td>7</td><td>8</td><td>9</td><td>10</td><td>11</td><td>12</td><td>13</td></tr>
<tr><td>14</td><td>15</td><td>16</td><td>17</td><td>18</td><td>19</td><td>20</td></tr>
<tr><td>21</td><td>22</td><td>23</td><td>24</td><td>25</td><td>26</td><td>27</td></tr>
<tr><td>28</td><td>29</td><td>30</td><td>31</td><td></td><td></td><td></td></tr>
</table>

MONDAY 18

TUESDAY 19

First Quarter Moon ◑

WEDNESDAY 20

You deserve a longer letter than this; but it is my unhappy fate
seldom to treat people so well as they deserve.

~Letter to Cassandra, December 24, 1798,
from *Letters of Jane Austen* (1884)

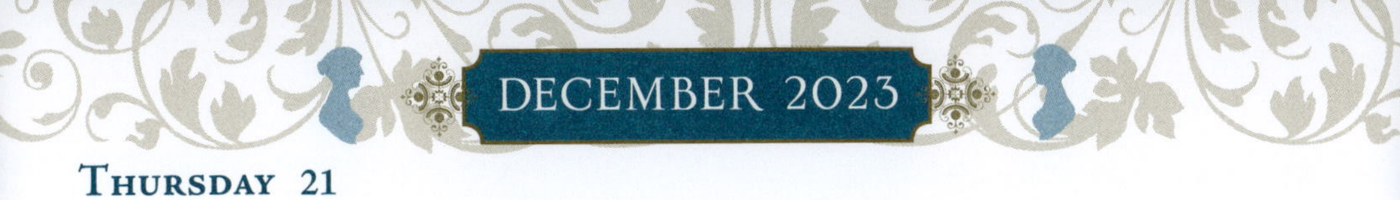

Thursday 21

Friday 22

Saturday 23

Sunday 24

November 2023

S	M	T	W	T	F	S
			1	2	3	4
5	6	7	8	9	10	11
12	13	14	15	16	17	18
19	20	21	22	23	24	25
26	27	28	29	30		

December 2023

S	M	T	W	T	F	S
					1	2
3	4	5	6	7	8	9
10	11	12	13	14	15	16
17	18	19	20	21	22	23
24	25	26	27	28	29	30
31						

January 2024

S	M	T	W	T	F	S
	1	2	3	4	5	6
7	8	9	10	11	12	13
14	15	16	17	18	19	20
21	22	23	24	25	26	27
28	29	30	31			

MONDAY 25

Christmas Day

TUESDAY 26

Kwanzaa, Boxing Day (CAN)   *Full Moon* ○

WEDNESDAY 27

I hope I shall remember, in future . . . not to call at
Uppercross in the Christmas holidays.

~Persuasion (1817)

DECEMBER 2023

Thursday 28

Friday 29

Saturday 30

Sunday 31

November 2023						
S	M	T	W	T	F	S
			1	2	3	4
5	6	7	8	9	10	11
12	13	14	15	16	17	18
19	20	21	22	23	24	25
26	27	28	29	30		

December 2023						
S	M	T	W	T	F	S
					1	2
3	4	5	6	7	8	9
10	11	12	13	14	15	16
17	18	19	20	21	22	23
24	25	26	27	28	29	30
31						

January 2024						
S	M	T	W	T	F	S
	1	2	3	4	5	6
7	8	9	10	11	12	13
14	15	16	17	18	19	20
21	22	23	24	25	26	27
28	29	30	31			

MONDAY 1

New Year's Day

TUESDAY 2

WEDNESDAY 3

Last Quarter Moon 

I can recollect nothing more to say. When my letter
is gone, I suppose I shall.

~Letter to Cassandra, January 7, 1807,
from *Letters of Jane Austen* (1884)

2023

January
S	M	T	W	T	F	S
1	2	3	4	5	6	7
8	9	10	11	12	13	14
15	16	17	18	19	20	21
22	23	24	25	26	27	28
29	30	31				

February
S	M	T	W	T	F	S
			1	2	3	4
5	6	7	8	9	10	11
12	13	14	15	16	17	18
19	20	21	22	23	24	25
26	27	28				

March
S	M	T	W	T	F	S
			1	2	3	4
5	6	7	8	9	10	11
12	13	14	15	16	17	18
19	20	21	22	23	24	25
26	27	28	29	30	31	

April
S	M	T	W	T	F	S
						1
2	3	4	5	6	7	8
9	10	11	12	13	14	15
16	17	18	19	20	21	22
23	24	25	26	27	28	29
30						

May
S	M	T	W	T	F	S
	1	2	3	4	5	6
7	8	9	10	11	12	13
14	15	16	17	18	19	20
21	22	23	24	25	26	27
28	29	30	31			

June
S	M	T	W	T	F	S
				1	2	3
4	5	6	7	8	9	10
11	12	13	14	15	16	17
18	19	20	21	22	23	24
25	26	27	28	29	30	

July
S	M	T	W	T	F	S
						1
2	3	4	5	6	7	8
9	10	11	12	13	14	15
16	17	18	19	20	21	22
23	24	25	26	27	28	29
30	31					

August
S	M	T	W	T	F	S
		1	2	3	4	5
6	7	8	9	10	11	12
13	14	15	16	17	18	19
20	21	22	23	24	25	26
27	28	29	30	31		

September
S	M	T	W	T	F	S
					1	2
3	4	5	6	7	8	9
10	11	12	13	14	15	16
17	18	19	20	21	22	23
24	25	26	27	28	29	30

October
S	M	T	W	T	F	S
1	2	3	4	5	6	7
8	9	10	11	12	13	14
15	16	17	18	19	20	21
22	23	24	25	26	27	28
29	30	31				

November
S	M	T	W	T	F	S
			1	2	3	4
5	6	7	8	9	10	11
12	13	14	15	16	17	18
19	20	21	22	23	24	25
26	27	28	29	30		

December
S	M	T	W	T	F	S
					1	2
3	4	5	6	7	8	9
10	11	12	13	14	15	16
17	18	19	20	21	22	23
24	25	26	27	28	29	30
31						

2024

January
S	M	T	W	T	F	S
	1	2	3	4	5	6
7	8	9	10	11	12	13
14	15	16	17	18	19	20
21	22	23	24	25	26	27
28	29	30	31			

February
S	M	T	W	T	F	S
				1	2	3
4	5	6	7	8	9	10
11	12	13	14	15	16	17
18	19	20	21	22	23	24
25	26	27	28	29		

March
S	M	T	W	T	F	S
					1	2
3	4	5	6	7	8	9
10	11	12	13	14	15	16
17	18	19	20	21	22	23
24	25	26	27	28	29	30
31						

April
S	M	T	W	T	F	S
	1	2	3	4	5	6
7	8	9	10	11	12	13
14	15	16	17	18	19	20
21	22	23	24	25	26	27
28	29	30				

May
S	M	T	W	T	F	S
			1	2	3	4
5	6	7	8	9	10	11
12	13	14	15	16	17	18
19	20	21	22	23	24	25
26	27	28	29	30	31	

June
S	M	T	W	T	F	S
						1
2	3	4	5	6	7	8
9	10	11	12	13	14	15
16	17	18	19	20	21	22
23	24	25	26	27	28	29
30						

July
S	M	T	W	T	F	S
	1	2	3	4	5	6
7	8	9	10	11	12	13
14	15	16	17	18	19	20
21	22	23	24	25	26	27
28	29	30	31			

August
S	M	T	W	T	F	S
				1	2	3
4	5	6	7	8	9	10
11	12	13	14	15	16	17
18	19	20	21	22	23	24
25	26	27	28	29	30	31

September
S	M	T	W	T	F	S
1	2	3	4	5	6	7
8	9	10	11	12	13	14
15	16	17	18	19	20	21
22	23	24	25	26	27	28
29	30					

October
S	M	T	W	T	F	S
		1	2	3	4	5
6	7	8	9	10	11	12
13	14	15	16	17	18	19
20	21	22	23	24	25	26
27	28	29	30	31		

November
S	M	T	W	T	F	S
					1	2
3	4	5	6	7	8	9
10	11	12	13	14	15	16
17	18	19	20	21	22	23
24	25	26	27	28	29	30

December
S	M	T	W	T	F	S
1	2	3	4	5	6	7
8	9	10	11	12	13	14
15	16	17	18	19	20	21
22	23	24	25	26	27	28
29	30	31				

NOTES

BIRTHDAYS AND ANNIVERSARIES

STERLING
New York

An Imprint of Sterling Publishing Co., Inc.

ISBN 978-1-4549-4587-1

Distributed in Canada by Sterling Publishing Co., Inc.
c/o Canadian Manda Group, 664 Annette Street
Toronto, Ontario, Canada M6S 2C8
Distributed in the United Kingdom by GMC Distribution Services
Castle Place, 166 High Street, Lewes, East Sussex, England BN7 1XU
Distributed in Australia by NewSouth Books
University of New South Wales, Sydney, NSW 2052, Australia

For information about custom editions, special sales,
and premium purchases, please contact
specialsales@sterlingpublishing.com.

Printed in Malaysia

2 4 6 8 10 9 7 5 3 1

sterlingpublishing.com

Cover Illustration by Kelly Thorn
Interior design by Gina Bonanno

Frontispiece: from *Jane Austen and Her Country-House Comedy*
by W. H. Helm, 1909; illustration from Violet Helm
Throughout: NASA/JPL-Caltech (moons); Shutterstock.com: N H art
(decorative border); valeriya_sh (decorative letters); Wikicommons (cameo)